The Party

A work of fiction by Andy Gilbert

Preface & Warning

I have the utmost respect for the Police and the work they do under the most trying circumstances throughout NZ and I really should emphasise that any similarity to any person living or dead, in this novel, is a sheer coincidence.

Further I should add that I have based this story in Rotorua as it is a town I know well. The story could be based in any town or city around New Zealand and I would go to great lengths to emphasize that comment.

Copying and using

The writer specifically withholds the rights to any reproduction in part or in whole of this work. Any such permission needs to have been given in writing by the Author and at all times the copyright of this work is retained by the Author.

Table of Contents

Chapter 1

I really don't know how I ended up here!

Okay, it's Mark Hammell here and let me remind you that I am a Detective Sergeant at Rotorua. What else do you need to know. Yes, I had an issue once with a WPC that thought it would be good for her career to be linked to a DS. It all ended not too well for me, and I swore off dating within the firm after that.

Okay, you all know I have a little guilty secret. I occasionally visit some of my working girls. I'd like to think that it's all part of my being in charge of the Vice squad but in reality, it's just easier to visit with a working girl and hand over a few dollars. One of my working girls is Janet. Janet is not your average girl doing it for the money or to fund her drug habit. Janet is that odd bod who just likes having sex with other blokes. Her hubby, Eric, is okay with that. In fact, I reckon it does him out of a job that might become a bit of a chore sometimes. You know what I mean.

Looking back, I had been visiting with Janet when she asked me to accompany her to an evening function. Straight away the short hairs on the back of my neck went up and I suggested she take her own husband to the event. She said he wasn't keen on going to this event for whatever reason. I told her I couldn't really be seen with a girlfriend as that would cause too many complications for me. So the next time I went to see Janet she had another go at me about going to this function. Only this time she was a little more circumspect when she asked me. Okay, she was doing something that she only did for special customers and that made it a little awkward to refuse. Come to think of it, I'd probably have agreed to do most things while she was busy treating me as if I was special. I stipulated, afterwards, that I could not be called anything related to my job. She assured me it was basically an invite out to a dinner function. It was to be held out in the country towards Hamurana and the dress for the evening was to be casual formal. She never drank so she would pick me up and I could have a drink or two if the evening was getting boring. What could possibly go wrong?

It was set for the following Friday evening. Janet knew where I lived so she picked me up and we agreed on a few details on the way out to Hamurana. It was a very pleasant day and the twilight was settling in when we got out past the golf course. It was probably nearing the time we put the clocks back. I should check when that is happening.

I have to say that Janet looked fabulous! She had a slim figure but was comfortably endowed in the top half, you know what I mean. She had put on a nice cocktail dress which showed off her curves well. She looked fabulous and I hoped I had dressed up to her standard. She had gone to some trouble telling me what I should wear which included her comment of "don't wear any of those suits you wear to work! They look ok, but I know they're still a bit tatty." My job for the evening, if anyone asked, was that I was in engineering as a rep. Mostly specialized stuff that I could palm off with a vague wave of the hand. My name was Mark, and I would fob off any further questions by asking what the person did for a living. I have to say that I had a few butterflies in my stomach. But what could go wrong, I asked myself as Janet drove us out towards Hamurana. We drove past the Golf club and then started looking out for the street numbers. It's an odd thing but you get close to a number and then you have gone past it. It's something to do with rural street markings, I am told.

The informality of the evening was pleasant, and I must admit I felt fairly relaxed as we mingled before dinner. There would have been perhaps ten people there, including Janet and I, plus the two hosts and as I sat down to dinner next to Janet, I was feeling a little more comfortable. It was a nice place and obviously there were a few dollars spent on the décor. It was that kind of place. The hosts had a table that would seat a dozen people. It definitely would not have fitted into my dining room but when you have lots of money like these people obviously did you could spend it on big dining tables and have lots of visitors around. It was a very pleasant mood around the table as the first course was brought in.

Life was easy when it was this relaxed. Janet and I were talking away, although the guy sat next to her kept trying to get her into conversation. When I eventually spoke to the lady sitting on my left side, she asked me if there was anything I was after. Now, normally I would be a beer drinker but as this was a little more upmarket, I went with a glass of white wine. She asked me if I was after anything special, and I replied that a nice glass of Chardonnay would be good. That was about the only white wine I knew about. She asked if I fancied something a little fuller bodied. In my innocence I asked if there was a chance for a brandy. Normally I would only get brandy at Xmas, but this seemed a little upmarket, so I was tempted to go for what was on offer.

She replied," Brandy, you mean the tart in the red dress. Yes, they always seem to go for her. I hear she is quite full bodied and so very obliging."

I laughed this odd remark away although I did think it was a strange thing to say about a fellow diner. When I turned back to Janet, she was looking a little bemused. I say that because I couldn't really work out what was on her mind, until she spoke.

She hissed at me from behind her hand," This is a bloody swingers do. One of those sex parties. It's a bloody wife swapping thing!"

My first reaction was, "Oh." My second reaction once I thought about what the woman on my left had said was "Oh, shit!"

Janet and I had a muffled conversation which was hissed at each other.

"The bloke next to me has asked me what position I prefer. That's not good!"

"That explains it. The woman next to me asked if I wanted something fuller bodied and suggested I hook up with the bird in the red dress. What do we do now?"

At that moment the host for the evening suggested that if anyone would prefer a little rest before the next course, the bedrooms were through the hallway and upstairs. Two couples who definitely did not come in together, disappeared into the hallway.

Laughter and chatter went on seemingly uninterrupted by the sudden disappearance of these two couples. Now for a fairly usual type of guy, I was at a loss what to do next.

Janet and I were at our polite but worried best.

Janet hissed at me, "Get us the hell out of here!"

My reply was not well received, "You're the bloody expert. You get us out of here!"

"I'm not going upstairs with any of these Tossers."

It must have sounded a bit odd to people who were regulars at this kind of party. Janet and I talking in a hushed whisper, kind of way.

"Me either, any ideas?"

"Wait for the next serving. Worst comes to worst, me and you will go upstairs and then we'll get out of here."

My automatic reply was stifled, fortunately by me. What I meant to say was that the meat course would be the next one on the table. It was not entirely appropriate, and I managed to change that to "Well, keep up the chat with me. and we'll play it by ear."

Janet and I were both being tried with conversation from the people sat immediately next to us. We did our best to keep up the flow of conversation, but it was not easy while we were trying to get out of the room. All along Janet and I kept repeating these conversations to each other.

"He's just asked me if have any no-nos. As in any positions I don't like."

"Well mine has just asked me if there is anything I might like that you won't go along with."

Janet looked a little amused, "Well, is there?" I reckon she was being serious!

My reply was that was not funny. Within a few minutes both couples who had gone upstairs reappeared and the next course was served. It's odd to be so casual with such a taboo subject as sex. But that is what the general gathering succeeded in doing.

During our conversation the guy opposite me said something to the effect of, "First time? Just relax and go with the flow. You never know, you might enjoy it. I think your wife is going to enjoy herself."

I touched Janet on her thigh, underneath the cover of the tablecloth, but it was only to stop her from replying sarcastically to the guy opposite. Yes, there was the odd time when Janet could be a touch sarcastic, and I did not want her to give full rein to her thoughts!

During the meat course the lady on my left enquired if there was a favourite thing I liked to do. She reckoned she would give anything a go. My reply to her was that was very obliging, but it seemed a bit lame to me. I have to be honest and admit that I was completely out of my depth in this group. It seemed odd that something we do so naturally should be so out in the open and being discussed like we were talking about the weather for this time of year. At least Janet and I thought it was a bit odd.

After the main course the invitation to 'go and rest' before the next course was repeated. Neither Janet nor I took advantage of this invitation Although there were three couples who did. It might be my occupation, but I did notice that one of the first couples who were quick to leave the room were both with different partners. A fact that Janet also commented on.

"That bird with the blue dress could get a room next to mine in Malfroy Road if she's giving it away that easy."

I declined to comment further as I was still trying to figure out how Janet and I would get out of the room.

Once the next course had been served, the dessert course, it seemed that the whole room were waiting to see who Janet and I had selected as our partners for the evening. Janet took the initiative by grabbing my hand and saying we were going for a rest before the brandy was offered.

Yes, we ended up upstairs.

Yes, we walked into the first available bedroom.

No I did not get naked, which was the first thing Janet started to do. I have to say she had on some really nice underwear, way better than her usual fare. And I have to say I quite liked what she was wearing. It was something I would have preferred to undress her from, if you get my meaning.

She said," Come on then. You might as well make the best of it."

I was naturally suspicious, "They might have cameras in the room."

"So turn off the lights and get undressed." She said this as she hopped into bed, giving me the briefest of peeps at her nudity. So now I was well tempted to get with what everyone else seemed to be up to. Oh, it can be quite a hard job when you are charged with being the nation's moral watchdog, as it were.

My suspicions were on full alert," They might have infrared cameras. Have you thought about that?"

Her reply was quite succinct, "Mark, if you don't get naked and get into bed, I'm quite likely to leave you here and go and get one of those idiots from downstairs to work with."

I turned the lights off, undressed and got into bed.

Janet's comment was, "That's better, now what did you say to that tart who asked you if there was anything I wouldn't be okay with?"

There actually was one thing I had never asked Janet for. We tried it and didn't like it much, so we consigned it to the 'let's not bother with that again' and went back to our usual way of passing the time. Am I wrong to say I quite enjoyed the somewhat less inhibited Janet? Well I did! She almost seemed like someone else as she suddenly got quite demure and coy. I wondered if anything was wrong but I then twigged that she was playing a game with me. I quite liked this game! Usually she was quite dominant. Tonight she was demure.

Eventually when we felt the time was right, we made it back downstairs to the dining room. Let's say the best part of an hour had elapsed. There were a few people sitting back having a post something or other brandy etc. Janet and I were ready to leave, having satisfied what we believed were our obligations. The host and hostess were nowhere to be seen and we could only assume they were upstairs in the arms of someone else. It might even have been their second time upstairs but that was not for me to worry about.

We said our farewells to the people gathered in the dining room and made our way out to Janet's car.

Once we were on the road, we started to have a giggle. I asked Janet who had invited her to the evening's festivities.

"The guy sat next to Brandy; she was the one in the red Dress. He comes to see me occasionally at Malfroy Road. Evidently, it's a fairly regular thing although they do have it at other people's places, but I swear he never said it was a swinger's thing. He said it was a nice evening with after dinner talk. He invited Eric and I. Eric would have died if we'd turned up there. He really doesn't go for all of this sex stuff. So thank you for showing up and going through with it.

I remember thinking as we passed the Hamurana Golf Course again that I counted myself as at home. Yes I had grown up in the streets of Manchester but as we went past the golf course and I could see the lights of Rotorua, across the lake, I felt somehow that I was at home and I was also helping make the streets of Rotorua safer. Somehow I belonged here.

We had a bit of a laugh on the way home. Janet dropped me off at my place and went home. I'd had a fairly good evening once I accepted the situation for what it was. I'd been propositioned by a very attractive lady. No, Make that two ladies. Brandy had made her way over to me and definitely showed some interest in me, and I'd had sex in a strangers bed. That has to count for something. No, I'd be counting this evening as a win. A good win.

Chapter 2

Saturday

One of the items that had been changed over the last few months was that we now had to cover Saturdays. I believe it was the CI's idea. Oh, did I mention that the ACI had been made permanent. As in, with all the hoo-hah with the case with the 'Panel' he'd been made the permanent Chief Inspector. As I said, it was the Chief Inspector's idea that one of us had to cover or be in for the Saturday during office hours. The Sarge was excluded from that duty but the rest of us had to be in a roster system for Saturdays. We all thought it was an excellent idea and I am sure the Boss would have fought it but that's what we ended up with.

As luck would have it, the day after the dinner was my Saturday on duty. I would usually manage to fill in the day by catching up on paperwork along with sorting out the myriad details of petty crimes that happened in a place like Rotorua. When I got in at just before 8am, I wandered over to the library café and got my coffee. Annie was not in today so someone else served me. I walked back to the front office door and let myself in, then settled down with my coffee and thought about what had happened the previous night. I was still fairly chipper about it all. Yes, it could have been embarrassing if I'd seen anyone that I knew, but that hadn't happened. I'd been approached by a couple of ladies who thought I was interesting. Interesting enough to perhaps proposition me. For a middle to late forties bloke I reckoned I was still in reasonably good shape, and Janet had not been disappointed in my efforts. All in all a pleasant evening was had by me.

I was still chuckling at the memory when the phone rang.

The Squaddies had a report of a body being found hanging, out towards Hamurana. The Squaddie had noted it didn't seem all kosher so could the CIB go and cast an eye out over the details. Looking around the office it dawned on me that I was the only lad available, so I said I would be there in a half hour. Apologies, I then sat down and enjoyed my coffee before heading out. By 8.30 I was on the road, having tucked in my camera and notebook and noted the number for the fingerprint lads if they were needed.

Driving out to Hamurana I realised that it was probably at least six months since I had been out to Hamurana. Other than last night, that is.

Hamurana is, to me, the back half of Lake Rotorua. It's the twenty odd kilometer stretch that the marathon runners do before turning back towards Rotorua. The street numbers go for a while and then you have to keep figuring out whether you have gone too far and is it ok to do a U turn in a narrow country lane.

Eventually I found the place and turned into the driveway. A nice place. Probably posh. Definitely whoever owned the place had a few dollars, judging by the quality of cars parked. I saw a BMW and a Lexus parked in the garage, so I knew I was coming to a money place. There was also a quad bike and one of those ride on mowers in the garage. When I look back I reckon it must have been a six car garage. Yep, this place smelled of money.

I carried on up the driveway until I found the Squad car and then I got out of the car and wandered up to the house, where the Squaddie was. I'd met the Squaddie once or twice in the Police Pub. The Police Pub was the social club where we could get a drink without being bothered by Rotorua's finest and we could get a drink upstairs in peace.

Greeting him, I asked what he had got for me.

"Male, probably late forties. Starker's. Hanged himself in the kitchen. Something didn't seem right, so I thought I'd better get you guys in to check it out. Dead on arrival so I left him where he was.

Widow is proper upset. She discovered him when she came down for a coffee this morning."

"Thanks, Steve. Ambulance on its way for the morgue?"

"No. Thought I'd leave the whole thing for you to tidy up. Best not have it swept up before you got here."

I walked into the house and alarm bells started to ring. I knew this place. Where from? Please appreciate that there are a whole raft of things going on in your head when you come across a murder or a body. I checked the body. Been dead for hours and quite stiff with rigor mortis so nothing there. Only at this point did I realise the guy was naked. Yes, the Squaddie had mentioned it, but I didn't quite register that fact. I didn't recognize him at first glance. It was only when I went into the next room, the dining room, that I remembered where I'd seen the bloke. This was his own house, and the last time I'd seen this victim was when he had been escorting Brandy or some other bird out of the dining room and up the stairs. I'd only been there the previous evening and enjoyed this bloke's cooking and his idea of hospitality.

By now alarm bells were ringing loudly in my head. The biggest alarm was that I should not be here! Firstly, I might be a murder suspect, however remotely. My second thought was who did I ring to get me out of this mess. I should ring the Sarge as he would know what to do. Then I knew I would have to ring the DI, my boss, with the hope that he would not have to inform the CI. I went and sat outside while I rang the Boss.

Apart from praying that he would answer, I also wanted him not to answer. When you're desperate you cling to anything.

He did answer the phone after it rang ten times. I could imagine him having a lie in, and this would not help his mood.

'Hello.'

"Hi Boss, It's Mark, DS Mark Hammell. I have a body out in Hamurana, and I might need you to have a look at it."

'It's Saturday morning. I'm having a lie in. Do I need to add bugger off?'

'Boss. I really need you to take lead on this one.'

'Why?'

I'm desperate for the boss to come but I really didn't want to say everything about the previous evening. That would, no doubt, come out later.

"Because there is a chance I may know the victim. Conflict of interest and all that.'

The Boss may have said something that was unprintable but it's sufficient that he did say he would be there in a half hour or so.

The Squaddie was surprised that I was done with my inspection so quickly. I told him I'd prefer to get the Boss involved so we should leave the scene untouched. I might have gone on about the Boss being in charge of all murder enquiries. Steve, the Squaddie looked at me a little oddly. Perhaps I was rabbiting on a bit much about the Boss.

I told the Squaddie he could go, and I would look after the crime scene. He left and I spent the next half hour practicing what I was going to say to the Boss.

Well I spent the next ten minutes practicing, then the widow came out, fully dressed but not as well dressed as I had seen her last night.

"Mm, it's Mark, isn't it. What are you doing here?"

"It's Detective Sergeant Hammell if we are being formal, Lesley."

"Oh? So last night you were not telling the whole truth? And Your wife?"

"Uh, girlfriend."

"Well, I should tell you about how I found Eric."

"Maybe you could leave it until the Boss arrives. Uh, he always prefers to hear it firsthand."

Lesley was quick on the uptake.

"Oh. Now I've got it. So, you might also be a suspect. I shouldn't really speak to you at all." She was upset but still a little amused at the coincidence of me being the first on the scene from the cop shop.

Fortunately, the Boss arrived at that point. I went over to his car, and he was not a happy chap!

"Alright, Detective Sergeant. So you've got me out of bed on my day off! This had better be good. In fact, it had better be damned good!"

"Okay, Boss. The widow is that lady there. Perhaps I should go back to the station and cover the office while you tidy things up here. You know, conflict of interest and things like that."

To be honest it even sounded lame to me that I had to get the Boss out to cover up for what was a poor choice of activity for Janet and I.

The Boss looked at me oddly. "Okay, DS. You go and spend the day in the nice warm office while I spend my day off tidying up this mess. Off you go."

I reckon the Boss might have wanted a bit more of an explanation, but I was already filled with dread about what had gone on the night before, so I was well ready to leave. I left quickly before the Boss got a chance to be just a little sarcastic with me. That I would leave for later and I knew that moment would arise. I headed back to the office. Obviously, I was going to cop it later, but I had at least followed the correct procedure by calling in the Boss and had done my job.

I returned to the temporary offices of the CIB, having stopped off on the way for another coffee. I wondered about ringing Janet up and telling her what had happened, but I thought better of it. No doubt the Boss would be wanting to have a chat with Janet, so I'd better not try to corroborate stories. I sat and tried to get on with paperwork, but my mind was going full tilt about how much trouble I would be in. Yes, I know I had done nothing wrong, but, in my fevered brain, this was the perfect excuse for the big Boss to get me transferred.

It would have been twelve thirty or so before the Boss came in. He walked into his office and shut the door. After ten minutes on the phone he invited me into his office. I walked in and he held the door open for me to walk past him. I could almost hear the cell doors clanging behind me as I walked over to the chair. It's an odd feeling when you truly know you have done nothing wrong but there is always a chance you might be found out doing something.

He slowly walked back behind his desk and sat down before he spoke. He looked at me for a few seconds with his hands up around his chin and said, "The Full story. That's what I want. Nothing left out. Assume I know nothing and you're making a full confession to me. Away you go, Detective Sergeant!"

Everything I had so carefully prepared to say just left me.

"Well, this girl and I were invited to this dinner party, only it turned out to be a swingers type of party. You know swapping partners and all that. We were surprised, but when we tried to get out without saying anything it was impossible so we went upstairs together and then we went home."

"And the girl's name?" the Boss demanded.

"Uh, is that really necessary."

"Her name!"

"Janet."

"Well that wasn't too hard was it. So you and Janet. Is this Janet from the motel, in Malfroy Road?"

"Yes." How the hell did he know that?

"May I ask what you were up to going to a wife swapping party with Janet?"

"I didn't know it was a bloody wife swapping party. Neither did Janet."

"So you and Janet were invited to this party. It turned out to be a swingers do, and you bottled it. I assume that you went upstairs with

Janet and then you slipped out the back door when you had done the deed. That sound about right."

"Yes, Boss. Oh and Janet and I left at the same time because we were in her motor. Maybe we left at around 11.pm."

I stuttered to a stop. I realised I was giving out too much info which the Boss was probably not interested in. That and the fact that the more you say at a time like this can be used against you. Not necessarily in a court of law but you know what I mean.

"Okay. You don't appear to have done anything wrong. Obviously, you're now a suspect in a murder case until I dismiss you as a person of interest. It's funny. If it was me, I'd have probably gone with Tiff. Asian birds are right up these swingers' alley. Although I must admit that Janet does dress up very nicely."

"What, is that it?" I could barely believe my ears. "And how did you know about Janet?"

"You're in charge of the Vice squad, that's one. Janet is certainly a very nice-looking lady and her hubby doesn't give a toss. Maybe it gets him out of the job. That's two. Third one is I've known about you and the girls for the last two or so years. It's part of my job knowing what my dicks are up to. Can I ask a question"?

"You're doing the interview," was about all I could reply. I thought I'd been so careful with my visits.

"The Sarge and I have a bet on. I reckon you're also visiting Sharon and the Sarge reckons it is Maureen from the Club."

"Well you're both wrong!"

"So who is it then?"

"Angel."

I have to say that I immediately regretted confirming their thoughts. There are some things that are private and well, I didn't really think it was something they would or should know about.

The Boss did say 'nice' but then had a thought about the case.

"Okay, so here's how we handle it. Firstly you take my Saturdays for the next couple of months. Secondly you are still on all duties except for this murder case, and it is a murder case. Thirdly, I dunno, I'll think of something. Now I have to interview these suspects. That will keep me going for the next day or so. Maybe I'll take a day off midweek. I'm sure you won't mind covering for me. Oh and you might as well bugger off home. I reckon you'll appreciate a day off when you're covering my Saturdays."

I took my leave and left for the day. Around 4pm the Boss rang and said he would need Janet and I to be available for an interview the next day. Would 10.30 be convenient. The way he said it, I had better be there with Janet. I of course agreed and then got to ringing Janet to make sure it was ok with her. Fortunately it was and then she asked me a bunch of questions about the case. I suggested that we should leave it to the DI to ask the questions. I think we might have had our very first argument at that point. She said she would see me at the office at 10.30 and hung up on me.

I have to say, being on the other side of the fence was a whole new experience for me. By that I mean being a suspect. The questions I would have asked, the Boss would ask slightly different questions. I tried to figure out what questions the Boss would ask. When I came up with nothing more than what I would ask, I went to bed. I must have slept for a while but as far as I am concerned, I had a sleepless night!

Arriving at the office in the morning, I hung around outside waiting for Janet to arrive, fortunately she was fairly punctual, so we walked in together and presented ourselves to the Boss.

When the Boss took a look at me, he laughed, "For god's sake, you've done nothing. Relax, Mark!"

Janet started talking, fast, and the Boss stopped her. He only wanted to hear her speak once we were sat in his office. We went and sat in the Boss's office and then the Boss started asking his questions. One thing I did learn that day was the best way to ask questions if you believe the person you are talking to is innocent. Be polite and kind. I have to say that the Boss was very kind with the two of us.

"Okay. I'll keep you both together. One of you start telling me what happened on the Friday evening, and spare me the details on what you and loverboy did together."

I started in as professional a way that I could until Janet interrupted with a point.

I started again and Janet also had another point she wanted to make.

In the end the Boss suggested I make a start and Janet would be asked questions later. In actual fact the Boss said that if Janet did not shut up he would interview us both separately and Janet would have to go second. That shut her up for a few seconds, at least.

I went through my story in as full detail as I could. Eventually the Boss asked me to make a seating chart where everyone was sitting at the table.

On the far side of the table and down towards the end:

"Opposite and down the end of the table was, Brandy."

Janet interrupted again, "She was wearing a nice dress; I'm going to say it was probably brought at an upmarket place. Probably Rose of Hamilton. I've brought stuff from there before and it's always very chic. Nice figure but probably putting on a few pounds as the dress seemed a little tight. She was upstairs with anyone who wanted to go upstairs. Oh, sorry."

"Next to her was a guy called Anthony,"

Again Janet interrupted," Odd sort of bloke. I think he was with Brandy but was definitely looking for a bit outside the marriage. Can I say he's visited me a couple of times? Very tidy in his dress and probably expensive too. Likes things a bit kinky and not above making suggestions."

When I looked at her she came to a stop, and she looked at me as if to say 'What.'

"Next to her was the bird in the long dress."

Again Janet interrupted, "Her name was Lorraine. Wearing a long dress to that kind of event is a no-no. Takes too long to get on and off and there's always the risk of a tear if you're in a hurry. If you ask me I'd reckon she was always in a bit of a hurry. That's the type of bird who'd cut notches in her bedhead to signal the amount of blokes she has bonked."

She then prodded me to continue.

"Next to her was, I'm going to say Michael. He was the one who spoke to me about it being our first time."

I looked at Janet for her comments, but she had nothing to say. Then she blurted out, "Probably compensating for a small dick. There's something about him that didn't add up."

"Next to him was Angela."

Again I waited for Janet to say something. She did not disappoint me.

"I liked her. She was quite chatty early on when we were mingling. Nice dress and nice makeup. Probably a hairdresser but that's a guess. She went upstairs with Anthony. The second time she went upstairs was with the host. Each time she came down, her makeup was immaculate. Sorry. Was I speaking out of turn?"

I looked at the Boss and he said nothing. I remembered then that this was his style. Let the suspect or whatever talk themselves out and then give them a prod.

"So carry on, DS."

"Next to Angela was the host. Name of Eric. He went upstairs with Angela once and when we came down, he was upstairs with someone else, probably."

I turned to Janet and waited. I was not disappointed.

"I could not have fancied him. Something about him gave me the chills. I reckon he was more for the women and giving them the pleasure. What?"

"So that was where our murder victim was sat. Stands to reason with him being the host, I guess. Please carry on, one of you."

"Thanks for your input on our host, Janet. Next to me was Becky."

Janet interrupted, again, "Probably not her real name. I noticed when some asked her something she didn't reply until she was asked again. Probably a bit too fond of booze. She was getting a bit blowsy with her weight. The dress she had on was a bit tight. That's usually a giveaway that she's struggling with her weight. She definitely fancied you, though, Mark. She was all over you until you realised where we were and started telling me to get you out of here. Give her fair due, though. She did keep trying for you. All that stuff about is there anything your bird was a bit iffy on. Yeah, I reckon she was right into you. I reckon you'd have definitely been in with her if you wanted. She had that air about her. Ready for anything and anybody."

I was just a little embarrassed, but I continued, "Then there was Janet and me. Next to us was another couple. Robin and I never got her name."

Janet continued to fill in the gaps.

"Oh, that was Robin and Estelle. They have a place a few kilometers down the road from where we were. It's towards that resort place, I forget the name. Sorry, I quite liked her, but he gave me the creeps. There was something about him that didn't add up, and no, I can't put my finger on it."

"Are you done, Mark?" asked Janet. I nodded.

"Right!" said Janet, "Let's get down to who was bonking who."

"What about the guy sitting at the end of the table?" asked the Boss.

Janet interrupted, "That was Lesley. She was an odd one. At first, I couldn't tell if she was a he, but by the time it was over I'd put her down as a she. Very mannish in her style. Suit. A nice suit if I'm being honest but I'd have to say it was a man's suit. She went upstairs with a bloke first. Micheal, if I remember right. The next time she went upstairs was with the group of four who left after the second course. Now here's where it gets a bit interesting. When she came back downstairs, she had lipstick on her face."

"And is that a bit odd?" said the Boss.

"It gets better," Said Janet. "Brandy was wearing the lipstick. It's called 'Knights in White Passion'. Quite expensive, but here is where it gets a bit interesting, when the group of four came down I noticed that both Lesley and Eric had Brandy's lipstick on their face. I reckon they all went up together and had a foursome."

"Can you remember who the fourth person was?" asked the Boss.

Janet looked apologetic," Sorry, I was too busy concentrating on the fact that Lesley and Eric had Brandy's lippie on their faces. It's something I've always fancied trying but never had the nerve. It's a shade of silver almost gray. I meant to ask Brandy if I could try it on, but I never got around to asking her. Is that important?"

The Boss just said, "Everything's important until we decide it isn't."

"Hang on!" I interrupted Janets recollections. " Lesley was sitting across from me at the table, across from me and one up. She was up next to Eric, wasn't she?"

Janet had a reply, "Get with the game, Mark. Lesley was sitting next to Eric before she went upstairs with Michael. When she and Michael got back, she sat down in Art's chair at the other end of the table. What's her name, Angela, was also sat next to Eric for a while. When Art got back, he went and sat next to Eric. Oh, so that's it. Art and Brandy went upstairs together." She looked at the Boss. "Sorry, is this confusing you?"

The Boss said, "Okay. I think I've got everyone who you reckon was, what? Can I use the word bonking if no one is offended."

I didn't have any opinion and Janet said it was fine.

The Boss continued, "Like I was saying. I think I have got everyone who was bonking that you two know about. Now I just have to work out with the rest of them who was bonking whom and when. I don't reckon jealousy was a part of it, but I still have to check it out. Right, Detective Sergeant, you can take the rest of the day off while I continue with my enquiries."

Then the Boss smiled at me, "You do know I'll get you back for this, don't you?"

My reply was, "I kind of figured that one out for myself."

"Right, off you both go. And take a rest. It can't be easy putting up with all of this bonking." That was said as he turned to walk towards the door. It was a definite dig and I assumed it was meant for me!

Chapter 3

M onday

It was Monday and it was another glorious late summers day. Warm and sunny. I didn't actually give a hoot about the weather because at 5 am it dawned on me that I hadn't told the Sarge. Not only had I not told the Sarge, but I was also going to be the subject of a few digs in the ribs when the two DC's knew what had happened. Yes, as you can imagine, I didn't sleep that well. The Boss and the Sarge were already in the office when I walked in. It wasn't my turn to get the coffee so I nipped in and closed the door of the Boss's office,

"Um, Boss?" I started and the Boss cut me off.

"You're worried if I told the Sarge and how will the two DC's take it if you aren't allowed on the case. Yes, they will probably assume something is amiss. They're not that thick! So here's what I'll do. I reckon you owe it to the Sarge to tell him but then again. I reckon I should be the one to tell the story. As for the DCs I'll put another name in for you and Janet. Fair enough?"

"Thanks, Boss"

"And you'll let me tell the Sarge? Come on, you at least owe me this one."

The Sarge walked into the office and handed me my coffee. The Boss asked him to shut the door and take a seat. From my face, I reckon the Sarge knew that something was up. Although he did not know what it was. I reckon my face was a mix of righteous indignation at having my activities discussed and also there might have been just a little guilt at having my activities discussed.

The Boss explained the details of what had happened on Friday night. He still had not mentioned the murder victim at that point. Then he explained how we now had to handle the office on a Saturday. Then he explained that I was actually there on Friday night and then I was called out to the scene of the murder on Saturday.

The Sarge thought the whole thing was hilarious. Then he realised that I had been involved on both Friday and Saturday. Sarge was now having one of the best days of his professional life ever! I held on to my look of righteous indignation and then the Sarge spotted me looking away and burst out laughing again,

Then the Boss finished with, "And our DS is visiting with Angel, so we're both wrong."

The Sarge was still laughing. "So you and who else went to this place?"

The Boss replied. "Janet, from the motel in Malfroy Road."

Again the Sarge had a fit of laughter but he did add that Janet was nice and dressed up very well. What is it about my sex life that others find so damn Interesting!

The Boss continued to say, "I don't reckon it will be great for morale if we let on that the DS is into wife swapping so I've arranged to put on the white board that the extra couple are Craig and Nigella. Maybe I'll put them down as an undercover team from Hamilton. That should work. Only you, me and the DS will know who the real person is. You okay with that?"

By now the two DCs were in, and the Boss called a meeting to discuss the events of the weekend. He pulled everyone together and we all sat down in random chairs to get his story.

"Right everyone. We have a murder case that I will be taking the lead on. Victim is one Eric Johnson, and I haven't got a pretty pic because the victim was found naked and I don't reckon it will be much good if a WPC walks across to our office and sees that. It seems they were hosting what I can only call a wife swapping party. Fortunately for us, we had a couple of undercover people from the Hamilton Office working on an unrelated case that were still on the job as it were. Okay everyone. Get your laughing out of the way. It's a murder case and we are serious about this."

I noticed Tim Cross had a big smile on his face and, annoyingly, the Sarge had a big grin on his face as well. I was pleased the Boss had worked an angle out for us being there without actually revealing to the rest of the Squad our true identities.

"Okay, I'll assume you have got it out of your chortles. So far, I have interviewed the widow, who was also there at the party, hosting. Interesting activity. As far as I can tell the victim owned four businesses doing plumbing in town, also in Tauranga, Taupo, and Whakatane. Seems he had just made the decision to become a gentleman farmer. He has a few hectares out at Hamurana, and he was going to have a go at stud farming. Reckoned he fancied having a go at Angus Longhairs, whatever they are. He could afford all the gear, so he was just building himself a cattle crush according to the widow. Has a quad bike and a ride on. He could well afford it. I've also interviewed the undercover cop couple and one other couple. I still have to tidy up interviewing the other three couples and I should have that done by today. The Detective Sergeant will cover my duties and allocate anything necessary as I want to try and get on top of this case. Sarge! If you can't stop giggling, you can go back to your deskwork."

The Sarge apologised and the Boss continued, "Right, any questions? See the DS and he will tell you what your day is going to be like."

With that the Boss went into his office. The Sarge went to his desk and the two DCs waited for me to allocate their duties. I ended up with an indecent exposure. I sent Tim to deal with a domestic burglary and Dave ended up with two cases: a burglary and an assault on a female.

I got back to the office around 11.00. My indecent exposure ended up a bust, and I ended up being the referee in a mini domestic. The

Indecent exposure was an odd case. The stepfather had walked out of the shower and 'accidentally' exposed himself to the teenage daughter. To be honest, a lot of my work seemed to end up with me being a referee and this was one of those cases. I couldn't quite work out if the teenager was looking for a reason to bust up the parents, but again I was only the referee.

The Boss was busy with people in his office. I thought it may have been Robin and Estelle from the party, by the look of the back of them, so I got out of the office and did some busy work for an hour. Turns out it wasn't them; it was Anthony and Brandy. She somehow looked different when she had her back turned and was hiding her most recognizable assets.

When I got back to the office, the Boss had done with his interviews, so I casually dropped in on him and equally casually asked if there was any progress. Well I believed I was being casual.

The Boss had other ideas, "I can't believe how many of these buggers bonked each other in a four-hour period. I shouldn't be questioning their jealousy. I should be questioning their stamina! I should have asked you first. I don't suppose there were any bowls full of Viagra handy on the table, were there?"

I had an idea that I was reluctant to put forward, but I had to anyway. It might have been relevant to the case.

"We left at er, well we were home by just after 11pm. Is it possible that the party went quite a bit later?"

The Boss was impressed, though he didn't show it. "Good thinking. We know you guys left at whatever time. Maybe it did go on till late. That would explain these middle-aged blokes' stamina. Oh and another thing. Neither of you mentioned Alain?"

I was a little surprised," And this Alain would be?"

"They're posh people with lots of money. Alain is their factotum. That's her words, the widow, not mine. He lives with them and cooks for them and looks after the grounds and stuff. It wouldn't surprise me if he was busy comforting the widow as we speak. I interviewed him. Well, as well as I could. Claimed he spoke very poor English. Cheeky sod asked me if I spoke French. As far as I could tell he has a place in the grounds, and he was gone before you left. I might get a French translator handy if I need to speak with him again."

At that point the Boss's phone rang.

"Hello.... G'day Mike......... You have the prelim on the victim. No. we'll come and see you."

With that, the Boss turned to me and spoke, "That was Mike from the morgue. Said he has the prelim report. You can come with me, but you also never saw the Morgue report. Okay?"

It appeared I was not allowed to speak about the case when I was actually an uncleared suspect. I didn't care. I was keen to see where this case went.

We got in the Boss's car and parked at the morgue exit. The Boss had a Police Business sticker for his car. I reminded myself to ask how he got that, but the Boss was all business and made his way into the morgue.

Mike, as always, was happy to see us. Anything with a bit of mystery to it was always up Mike's Street.

He had already started on his report when we got into the morgue.

"Subject was 44 years old and in good condition. Physically kept fit but showed signs of aging and the good life. Cause of death was probably strangulation. Until I'm told otherwise that is what I'm putting on the report. Note I said strangulation and not asphyxiation. I reckon the guy was strangled first and he was strung up to make it look like suicide. Time of death would be somewhere between two am and 4 am. Fortunately for you lads I was in on Saturday morning tidying up paperwork, so I was able to comfortably detect the approximate time of death. Another odd thing to think about. His assailant came at him from behind. That's what the bruises would indicate but with the bloke being strung up a lot of the bruises are covered by rope marks.

Now as to his general condition there's a little bit of liver deterioration, probably linked to a good lifestyle. Now I'd like to ask questions. Was this guy a bit of a party animal?"

The Boss replied that was a strong likelihood.

Mike continued, "I thought so. There are good signs he had sex with someone on the night he died. Possibly more than one person. I've got vaginal fluid in his pubic hairs, possibly from more than one female. I'm going to go out on a limb and say that this guy was into an affair, or he was into wife swapping."

The Boss replied that was a definite possibility. Mike looked at the Boss and then looked at me. Eventually the Boss let out a little more information.

"There is some evidence that he was up for a bit of wife swapping. But what makes you come to that conclusion?"

Mike replied, "All the evidence says that he was meticulous with his use of condoms, so there is effectively no DNA evidence worth anything other than that he used condoms. There is also strong evidence he had anal sex. This bloke was getting it from all ends if you'll pardon the pun. Now I have also sent for a tox report, but I think there is little doubt that he also had a drink or two before or during or after his sex. Possibly all three but I won't know that until the tox report gets back. Maybe tomorrow?"

The Boss was a little perturbed, "Thanks for getting on to it, Mike. Are you sure about the back door bit?"

"100% positive. And I might be going out on a limb here, but I'd say it was not his first time. There are signs of relaxed muscles which would indicate it wasn't his first time. How did you say it? Going in the back door?"

"Thanks again, Mike. That sort of opens up a bit of a can of worms for us, but thanks again for getting on to it."

Heading back to the station the Boss was quiet and deep in thought.

When we got back to the station, or our version of the station, the Boss called the Sarge and I into his office and shut the door.

He explained what Mike at the morgue had said. Then he waved his hand at us to indicate that he didn't really know where to go at this point. The Boss believed Mike's view about the strangulation being before the hanging but couldn't see what the point was. He liked to tidy things up and this did not add up.

The Sarge was quite practical, "Well you now have to re-interview all of the suspects and ask them about their homosexual tendencies. Did he exhibit them openly? Did anyone know he was bent? Did his missus know? She'd probably know about it before his mates would." The Sarge was very good at 'freeballing' which is where you let an idea come into your head and then run with it.

The Boss spoke, "Well I have already interviewed three or four of the couples so that leaves me with more questions to ask the last two and then I have to sit down with the first four and ask them more stuff. "

Turning to me he continued, "My oath, you got off lucky with this one, Mark. But I will get you back!"

I had to add something. I hoped it might be useful to the Boss and he would stop having a go at me. "You could also ask who was with who, and also when they actually left the victim's place. Might give you a bit more to work with?"

With that the Boss looked at his watch and said, "It's ten to four and I have the Nicholsons at four. That's Robin and Estelle to you. I'm not yet on first name terms with them!"

It may have only been my imagination, but I felt there was just an edge to his last remark as he swept out of the door.

Then I got a call from the Squad room. It was the desk Sarge and he suggested I think back a few weeks. Didn't I have a case where the perp had vandalized a cricket wicket? When I said yes he said I should get up to Malfroy School. My perp may have struck again. I went to the School and was met by the headmaster and we went over to see the grounds man. On inspection I knew my lad had struck again. This time it was the rugby pitch at the school and the idiot had only sprayed the area from the 22 yard line right across the pitch at one end and damaged most of the 22 yard area, with his careless application of some type of weed killer. I could tell by the distinctly brown tone of the grass in the affected area. I had seen the same thing happened at Otonga Road School and the other place. I knew what I had to do. I told the grounds man to fence off the whole playing area. He was happy to just fence off the 22 yard area but I knew it had to be completely fenced off. He was muttering under his breath as he stomped off. I got on the phone to the forensic lads and told them to bring their biohazard gear. I had a word with the headmaster and we discussed what had been done with the other cases. Hopefully we knew the grass would die off and have to be just re-laid but before then we had to have the forensics lads turn up and analyse the scene for what had been sprayed on the grass. With luck, we would know what been sprayed by tomorrow midday. There had been no game played on the pitch since last Tuesday. I suggested he advise the parents and anyone who may have walked even a dog across the area. They would need to be checked out. The grounds man had returned by now and I watched as he angrily went round the perimeter of the pitch area using ropes and stays to rope the whole thing off. The headmaster disappeared and I was left waiting for the forensic lads to turn up and I thought about offering to help the grounds man rope the pitch off. I thought better of that. If the grounds man was going to be so grumpy he could do it on his own. I noticed a pile of dog crap on the side of the pitch and I immediately wondered if this was what one of the finest brains in the local CIB was reduced to, checking for dog poo!

I waited for the forensic lads and watched for a while as they dug up a few areas of turf to take away for analysis. I didn't think they would work through the night to get their results as they had done with the Otonga Road case. As I stood and watched the forensic lads get on with their work the headmaster rejoined me and the head of the forensics team. I half listened as the forensics guy was explaining to the headmaster what the previous cases had incurred. I heard him say that the first case had involved an over the counter brand of weed killer but the second two had involved a stronger weed killer. The type you buy in a 5 liter jug or more. The results of the stronger brand were more significant. This type of weedkiller killed anything for up to six months and you would definitely need the pitch to be re-laid. Just then I noticed the grumpy grounds man walk up to one of the forensic lad and poke him on the shoulder. I decided to walk over and intercede before the grounds man needed to be arrested.

The forensic guy walked off the sprayed area and stood nearly at the halfway line and summoned the grounds man over to him. I increased my speed just a little. I didn't want this getting out of hand. As I approached the forensics lad was asking how the grounds man would know whether it was a group 5 defoliant the guy had sprayed, such as Agent orange. The grounds man said it was obviously not Agent orange. By this time I had arrived and was at the point of separating the two arguing. The forensics lad turned to me and said, "Detective Sargeant, it's possible this bloke knows what was sprayed on the pitch. I'd suggest you interview him and smartly before he buggers off." The grounds man was adamantly denying any knowledge of the crime. The forensics lad carried right on and said, "Well if you don't know what the hell they sprayed on the grass, you won't mind if I carry on and do my bloody job then, will you!"

With that he turned and walked back to the sprayed area of the pitch. The grounds man vehemently denied he had anything to do with the spraying of the pitch. I suggested he calm down and let the forensics lads do their thing. We walked off the pitch together and I explained that the forensics lads would need full gear if they didn't know what had been sprayed on the pitch. I calmed him down. When I turned back to the pitch the forensics team were packing up their samples and the headmaster looked worried as he would have to somehow alert any member of the public who had walked across the fields to get a checkup, just in case.

It was well after 5.00pm when I left. I had hoped the Boss would call me and fill me in with what the Nicholsons had said, but he evidently went straight home. Also he went to see the last couple once he had his tea, so when he came in the next morning, he was pleased about what he had come up with but still displeased that he had to work late that evening. It was still my job to hand out assignments from over the road that needed CIB input. I may have pulled rank and given all of the cases to the two DCs. I was going to pop in the Boss's office when he called me in.

<u>Tuesday</u>

The Sarge was busy attending to someone at the counter, so it was just the Boss and I.

"Right, I spoke to the Nicholsons and after that I went to see Michael and Lorraine. Our victim was a little bit secretive about his homosexual activities, but it was an open secret and most of the group were aware. So he liked a bit of backdoor stuff, and he was also partial to the ladies as well. This type of evening goes on once a fortnight according to the Nicholsons. Usually the same crowd but someone had left the district so that's why they invited Janet and her husband. Yeah, we know you turned up but that's by the by. As far as I can tell our victim was getting his jollies not only with the ladies, but also with Alain. Until I have a word with the widow I don't know if she was aware. But I do need to have another word with this Alain, so I'll have to get a translator in. That's more expense for the Boss but he'll have to wear it, this time. How about you? Have you or Janet remembered anything useful?"

"I haven't spoken to Janet since Sunday, and I haven't thought of anything since. Though, thinking about it now, I remember that Alain came into the dining room once. He had a word with the widow and then disappeared back out again. Sorry about that, there was so much going on and toing and froing it was hard to keep count of who was and wasn't there."

The Boss was a little surprised that I had not rung Janet at all.

"Well, give her a ring. Tell her in vague detail what we know so far and see if she remembers anything else. I tell you what, DS, if you're going to have a girlfriend you have to keep her better informed. Birds like that! Oh yeah, I hear from the Sarge you had another case with your bloke with the weed killer. No joy on that one?"

I was going to say that I didn't consider Janet as my 'bird', but I couldn't tell whether or not the Boss was joking, and I didn't want to give him that satisfaction. I did mention about the school weed killer and said I would have a look at that when I got time. He reckoned my first job should be to give Janet a bell. Birds like that from their bloke. He'd been married twenty odd years and his missus always appreciated it when he was going to be late.

Returning to my desk I gave Janet a bell. She picked up on the third ring and was quite pleased to hear from me. Okay, maybe chalk one up for the Boss.

I'd like to think the relationship I had with Janet was fairly professional. But she was obviously pleased to hear from me. She was quite warm and friendly on the phone.

"Hi, Mark. I was wondering if you were going to ring or when. Got anything new with the case?"

"There are a few things to note. Did you know that the victim was having a sexual relationship with the butler?"

Up till an hour ago I'd never even seen or heard of this butler, but Janet was one of those people that notice everything.

"The French guy? I kind of figured it out, and there was also the other bloke, what was his name, Art! That was it. He was the one sitting at the end of the table and when the host's missus came and sat in his place, he was quite happy to go and sit next to Eric. I reckon they were also doing the beast with two backs. It might just be me, but I wouldn't fancy having a go with a bloke that's also doing the blokes as well. Is it me or does it seem just a bit ...mucky?"

"I have to be honest and say that it doesn't do a lot for me either. I've never really thought about it but it doesn't have that much appeal. Maybe I'd better come and see you, give you a proper interview. At least I can pass some stuff onto the Boss."

Her parting reply was that I'd not be passing everything back to the Boss, "Would I?"

That gave me a little pause for thought. If the Boss and the Sarge both knew what I was up to in my sort of spare time, is it possible they had been there? Now you know what I mean, so don't get all coy. But it is something I should ask about, delicately?

I decided to re-interview Janet and made an appointment to call round.

In the interim I sat down with Dave and Tim. I asked them to back me up on the case of the weed spray if anything else happened while I was out at the murder investigation.

Obviously, Janet took our conversation the other way so was semi naked when I got round to her motel room. I was trying to be professional but it was too hard with the obvious distractions. Janet was trying to help me with the case but with her being rather unclothed, it made it very difficult to concentrate but I did manage to conduct an informal interview and came up with a few things to relate to the Boss.

I think the main thing was about Alain, and Janet's thoughts about him and Eric, the murder victim. It did confirm what the Boss was already thinking about Alain and Eric. As far as Janet was concerned the victim and Alain were quite likely to be getting it together. She also mentioned Art again as a possible suspect. She wasn't quite so certain about the victim and Art, but she did think there was something going on with them. There was something about the way they spoke to each other. An 'easy familiarity' she called it.

I was a little reluctant to pass on Janet's feelings to the Boss. Mainly because I didn't really want the Boss to be keeping a tab on my activities, but I did pass on the bulk of what Janet had said. As far as the Boss was concerned, it more or less confirmed what he had thought.

The Boss still had a couple or more re-interviews to sort out. He had one booked in for midday. He left for that interview, and we didn't really see him for a couple of days. I should say that when I was in the office, he wasn't, so we kept missing each other. Fortunately, the local paper had other things to report on so the case of some idiot spraying weedkiller was not reported in the local paper.

Thursday

Bright and early on Thursday I was into the office. Another late summer day with the promise of warm temperatures and close to a frost at night. Workwise, I firstly I had to deal with the stuff that wanted CIB attention from over the road. Annoyingly we had a couple of ram raids on dairies. Yes, we had had them before, but we were hoping it was a one off. If the local toe rags discovered how easy it was to make money out of cheap fags, we could be in for a bit of trouble.

The Boss called us all together for a summary meeting to report on what he had discovered about the murder to date.

He was impressed that such a bunch of old fogies could be up for so much sex in an evening. He was almost daring us to comment that the DI and I and the Sarge were also of that age group. No one dared to make the comment so, after a pause, he continued.

"On average I reckon they all had it three times, other than the Undercover lads from Hamilton."

Tim Cross made a comment/enquiry about what the undercover people from Hamilton would have gotten up to when they went upstairs.

The Boss was probably in one of his better moods because he asked me, "I don't know. What do you reckon they got up to, Detective Sergeant?"

As usual I was in a receiving info mood and to be made the centre of attention was not really what I wanted, "Oh, I don't know Boss. Maybe they just compared decoder rings?"

The Boss continued, "The DS reckons they probably compared ring sizes so that's what we'll go with. Right, I interviewed most of the people who went to the party for a second time. In fact I've done them all except the butler and he wants a translator, so I'll get to him later. My main source of enquiry has been to find out who bonked who. The DS and I will work out a list and then I'll get back to you lot. Right. It seems that we've had a couple of ram raids. I spent a week or so in Hamilton sorting this out, along with the DCs, so if we need to, we can probably get the Hamilton lads down here if it gets to be a nuisance. You two DCs will get onto the ram raids. See if you can spot a pattern developing. The DS and I will get onto the murder case. Any questions? Okay, so what are you hanging around here for?"

The two DCs sat at their desks for five minutes and then went out to continue their investigations. The Boss and I went into his office and settled down to sort out who had been bonking who at the party. The Boss asked me first If I had any leads on who was damaging the school pitches. I said I had no leads on the case. If it was three different schools it fairly ruled out a parent who was disgruntled. In all three cases the weedkiller had been the same. It was a weedkiller that was not used by the professionals and available in bulk quantities. It was the type of thing you purchased in a one or two liter bottle. Now I had further information that the weedkiller may be getting a bit more upmarket with the brand of weed spray, the Boss suggested I check the poison records. I already had my answer on that line of enquiry in that any poisons records would be of no use as only the better retailers kept a poison register. We got back to discussing the murder case.

The Boss started with, "I'm confused but here is what I reckon with the bonking."

"I reckon Michael bonked Becky and Brandy and Estelle."

"Lorraine, Michael's missus had it away with Anthony and Art and, I'm guessing here, It might have been Art, again."

"Anthony had it away with Lesley and Estelle and Becky. Just quietly I reckon that Becky could be a bit of a raver." The Boss's thoughts were wandering so I pulled him back to the topic.

"Brandy is Anthony's wife. She had it away with Lesley, Art and Robin. Lesley I am not sure about but I reckon she was a definite starter for the girls in the room. Another thing I have to say is that all of these birds were fairly fit looking, as in nice looking birds. Not often you get that when you get into the forties. Am I wrong in labelling them all in their forties?"

"You're probably right, Boss. Although they did seem a bit younger. Maybe it was the lighting that made them look good." The Boss was still thinking of them as ladies to have sex with and not as a possible murderer. Again, I dragged him back to the topic.

"Art Is Becky's boyfriend. She had it away with Lorraine and Estelle and Lesley. That's just my opinion but Janet reckons Lesley is into the ladies."

"Robin was sitting down next to Janet, and he is Estelle's hubby. He got away with Brandy and Lorraine and I think it was Becky."

"Estelle, as far as I can make out got off with Art and Michael and Eric."

"Lesley, she is the widow, also Eric's missus. I reckon she got off with Brandy and Becky and also Michael. It's a long list so I might have been mistaken, but I'm only getting this list because of what people who were left at the table were assuming. There's quite a bit of gossiping goes on with those who are still sat around the table about who is doing who upstairs."

"Becky, she is Art's girlfriend. I think she got off with Michael, Anthony and Robin. Can I say that for forty year old blokes they are all having sex with a bit more passion than I manage. We'll count them as having sex three times but I reckon we might be exaggerating their prowess just a bit?"

"You and your lady friend got it off with each other and I don't for a moment think you were comparing decoder rings! Oh and before I forget. There were a couple of ladies there who fancied a go at you. Becky and Brandy. There were also a couple of the blokes who wanted a go at Janet, so you might have left a bit early."

I was just a little pleased, "So there were a couple of the ladies that fancied me?"

Maybe it's a man thing but to know there were a couple of ladies who fancied you is not too displeasing but then the Boss sort of ruined it.

"Sorry to disappoint you, DS. That Lesley also fancied a crack at Janet so that makes her three and you two. Sorry about that, Mark, but you were looking a bit smug!"

The Boss didn't look that disappointed as he continued." So where do we go from here? All we have is a load of letches who got it off with other letches."

I added, as I felt it was expected of me," So you still have to re-interview this Alain again. Does anyone stick out to you as a possible suspect?"

"To be honest, none of them do! I've had my first 48 hours and a bit more and no one is jumping out at me!"

We discussed the case for perhaps another half hour before wrapping it up. The Boss reckoned I should sit in on the Interview with Alain. If I hadn't noticed him, there was a chance he had not noticed me. We teed up the interview for that afternoon and then we had to find a French translator who could come in with us. Suffice to say, we got it organised and I prepared myself for what was to be one of the oddest interviews I have ever been a part of. Odd in a very French sort of way.

Before that I received a call from Colin Handley, the police psychology guy He was based in Wellington but had an overview of anything happening in New Zealand. He introduced himself then started asking questions. Did I have any suspects in mind. On the first case we got a good spread in the local paper. Yet we had nothing on coverage for the next couple of incidents. Why was that? I ventured an opinion that the local paper had something else more noteworthy and would save the desecration of sport pitches it for a slow news day. In chatting we discussed the profile of the offender. Likely to be single or in a dead beat husband /wife relationship. Either way he could act on his own without being questioned. The psych guy reckoned the offender wanted publicity. He would probably try something more serious if he didn't get decent coverage. I said I would do my best with the local paper to get some coverage and we parted company. The psych guy was only giving me a heads up that the guy may try something more serious if he didn't get the publicity he felt he deserved.

I gave a call to the local paper and let them interview me for ten minutes. I did explain why I was calling so I was not surprised when the next day's paper came out with a fairly minor coverage of the event without even a photo of the damage done. The whole article covered a couple of hundred words across two columns. Maybe I had overplayed the element of getting coverage to make sure we didn't get a more serious crime, the next time.

Getting back to Alain's interview, it was set down for two o'clock. The Boss and I were waiting with the translator when in walked Alain to our temporary offices. The Sarge showed him through to the Interview room and we all sat down. So far so good.

The Boss started talking. He was doing the general pre-interview saying who was there etc. when Alain stood up and insisted, we have a translator present.

The Boss confirmed that the fourth guy in the room was actually the translator. The translator spoke a few words in French to confirm he was present and Alain sat down.

The Boss addressed his questions to Alain and the Interpreter did his job and repeated the questions to Alain in French.

Boss's question, "Do you understand why we are here conducting this interview?"

Through the translator, Alains reply was, "Yes, because you do not understand the French." It somehow seemed just a little disdainful, the way he said it.

"So how long have been a butler or factotum with the Johnsons?"

"I do not understand the question."

The Boss tried another tack. "How long have you been here in New Zealand?"

"I have been here in New Zealand for perhaps five years."

"And how long have you had a friendly relationship with the Johnsons?"

"I have been a friend with Eric and Lesley for perhaps four years."

"Have you ever been a part of a gathering such as happened last Friday night?"

"Yes. Of course. There is not every time a woman can bring her man."

"So can I assume you have had sex with New Zealand women?"

"Yes."

"Have you ever had sex with a New Zealand man?"

The translator was having some difficulty with his translation into French and there was a little bit of back and forth before the translator managed to get his answer out. Personally I think the translator was having some difficulty with the casual nature we were using to talk about sex with other people. And in the context of our conversation there was also the added mystery of perhaps homosexual sex between consenting adults. It was not a great day at the office for the translator.

"You Kiwis find it so hard to understand. I have had sex with many women and also it is possible I have had sex with men. In France it is all a part of friendship. Sometimes it may lead to sex and sometimes not. It is the same with women."

"May I ask if you ever had sex with Eric Johnson?"

"It is certainly possible, but I do not recall every time I have relations with someone. Who does that?"

As a listener to this conversation I could get what this Alain was trying not to say, and I could also gather what the Boss was trying to ask.

"Is it possible you may have had a sexual relationship with Mrs. Johnson?"

"It is possible, I grant you, but not something I would ever keep count of."

"Please consider your reply to this question carefully. Did you ever have a sexual relationship with either Mr. or Mrs. Johnson?"

Alain looked at the translator as if he was asking a very rude question. The translator repeated the question in very clear and well enunciated French.

"Yes, it is possible."

"How possible?"

"Yes, I suppose I have had a friendship with both of the Johnsons."

"Let me be very clear. A sexual relationship?"

"Yes."

"And of those people there on the Friday evening, how many of them did you ever have a sexual relationship with?"

"Inspector, there is a difference between a one-night stand and an ongoing relationship of this nature."

"Okay Alain. Have you ever had sex with Lesley. A one-night stand or something more regular?"

"Yes, and perhaps just a little more regular."

"Becky?"

"Yes."

"Estelle."

"No, or I do not think so."

"Lorraine? You don't seem to have commented on whether it was a one nighter or a regular thing."

"Yes. Perhaps a few times but perhaps not regular."

"Janet?"

"No."

"Eric?"

"Yes."

The Boss deliberately paused.

"With Eric, Yes and it was not, how you say, infrequent."

"Michael."

"No, I do not think so."

"Anthony?"

"No."

"Art?"

"Yes, I believe that is possible. Okay, the same as with Eric, perhaps?"

"Mark."

"No"

"Robin?"

"No I do not believe so. *Un Moment*. There may have been just the one time, but it was not his thing."

The Boss turned to me, "It's a pity I can't ask him if he is into that strangulation thing - auto asphyxiation or whatever they call it."

"No, that is not a thing I am into."

Even the translator was shocked at Alain's reply.

The Boss was ready with another question until he realised that Alain had just answered his question without the benefit of the interpreter.

"Hang on Alain. You just said that was not your thing. You said you barely spoke English. And here you are answering a very technical question. Perhaps an interpreter is not needed?"

Alain was quick to respond, "Maybe he should be here and maybe not. But if you are trying to set me for a murder, maybe he should be here, so I do not answer your questions incorrectly."

The Boss thought about it for a second or two. "Okay Alain. It is possible that you and I may have got off on the wrong foot. I am not here to trap you into the murder. That's not how the NZ Police do it. If you have done nothing wrong, you will be quite safe to speak with us. Perhaps we can talk with more direct questions. When did you leave the party on Friday night."

"When I cooked the dinner, I was let go. I went back to my room. I saw your friend here leave at around 10.45." So he had known that I was there. I really should pay more attention to my surroundings. Can I use the excuse that I had a drink? Perhaps not!

"And the other guests?"

"They left at various times I think the last one would have left a little before two in the morning."

"And that was it?"

"No. One car came back or was already there. I can say I did not hear a car in the driveway but perhaps I was asleep. This car was there for perhaps a half hour. That car left at perhaps 2.30 in the morning.

"Alain, was the car already there or did it return to the Johnsons?"

"I am not as certain as you would want me to be. Perhaps it was still there. Perhaps it was driven back again." This was finished with a gallic shrug as if to say why do you ask me all of these questions?

"Thank you. I don't suppose you saw who was driving the car?"

"Inspector. I had cooked a magnificent meal and been dismissed out of mind like a piece of rubbish or garbage. I too have feelings and I know what happens when the lights go on upstairs. To be dismissed without a care is not making me feel too good. I was happy when all the cars had left, and I could get some sleep."

The Boss turned to me and said," At last, we are getting somewhere!"

Turning back to Alain, the Boss continued, "Who found the body? Sorry, where were you when the body was discovered?"

"I was in my room. After these parties the Johnsons have a late morning before they awaken. I was already dressed as I was waiting for the summons to tidy the house. Is that correct? I heard Lesley scream at just before 8 in the morning. I rushed over but it was too late. Eric was already dead. They told me he strangled himself with a rope. That is correct? I had no idea he was depressed, that is the right word?"

The Boss did not enlighten Alain as to the real cause of death. He probably had his reason for that.

"Alain, we are still working on who committed the crime, if indeed a crime was committed. I'd like to thank you for your answering the questions and although we may still have further questions for you, at this point you are free to go."

Alain made a strange comment, "Anyone who is English will have an old view of sex. You are very conversative with your ideas."

The Boss was puzzled, "You reckon we are, what, chatty about sex? Sorry I don't understand you."

The translator stepped in, "I think he means you English are very conservative when you talk about sex. As in it's not something to be discussed."

Alain added,. "Yes, you English are very con-serv-ative when you talk about sex. Not like the French."

Alain stood up and shook the Boss's hand, then mine and the translator. I thought at the time that he may have had a prior run in with the French Police and they were not known for being quite so gentle when they had a suspect to interrogate.

Chapter 4

The Boss and I went back to the general office and the Boss called me into his office.

"Well I have done a bit of digging with this case. According to the files in the vast majority of these swinger or wife swapping party goers, the main cause of anything happening is jealousy. So if I have ten people who all swapped partners, I'm not counting you two in this case, I have up to ten suspects for doing this Eric bloke in."

I suddenly felt very brave. I don't know why. I asked the Boss, "Why do you know, or how do you know that Janet and I aren't suspects?"

"That's a very good question," the Boss replied." and here's my answer. Firstly you're a do gooder not a do badder. Crikey, even the Sarge knows what you are like. Secondly, I looked into your eyes, and I knew you hadn't done it. Thirdly Janet. She's a working girl and that's fine but if she thought she had done the slightest thing wrong she would be all over nervous. When I spoke to you two on Sunday, Janet was all for telling me who had possibly done it. If she had done it, she wouldn't be able to look me in the eye. And you also have a second question for me, don't you?"

"Not that I can think of."

"Well when you get the nerve to ask me, don't bottle it in. If you want an answer, the best way to get it is to ask the question. Ok? Right, as I was saying, I have nine suspects, ten if you include Alain. But something tells me he's not that kind of bloke. Let's start by saying what we know these people have in common. Then we can start to find what they don't have in common. That may give us a lead. What about you handle the whiteboard and I'll sit in my comfy chair. Oh By the way. You do know you're covering this Saturday, don't you?"

Glumly I acknowledged that I was well aware of my covering the Boss's shift on Saturday. Then we started on the whiteboard.

The Boss started with

'Rich!'

'A butler or factotum, whatever she called him!'

'Kinky!'

'Wife swapper!'

I added a few items.

'Remote location!'

'Set back from the road!'

'Lots of bedrooms!'

The Boss continued, "All fit birds, and the blokes as well! Crikey if they can go three times the blokes must be well fit!"

"Middle aged?" I added.

The Boss added, "Influential, in town? They'd have to be to get access to all of these swappers."

I added that we were calling it wifeswappers, but it seemed like the women were not what you'd call reluctant to participate.

The Boss agreed, "So the women were also a bit kinky with it. I like that."

We added a few more items, although the pace of suggestions had slowed down by then.

The Boss looked at the list and said, "Well they're fairly typical bored rich people who like to get a bit on the side."

My comment was that it didn't only apply to rich people. The Boss's response was that all of this lot seemed to be fairly well off. We agreed to differ.

The Big Boss interrupted our thoughts with his phone call. It seems he had been reading the local paper and he had read about the ram raids. It would also appear he wasn't happy with it and what were we doing about it? The Boss said we had already allocated a couple of lads to look at it and we were waiting for their report. I'm listening to this conversation through the earpiece of the Boss's phone. It seems that the big Boss wanted to know how I was handling it. When the Boss explained that the two DCs were doing the investigation he was not happy. When the Boss explained that the two DCs were probably the most experienced at this type of crime because of their work with the Hamilton operation, the big Boss was only slightly mollified. When asked what I was doing, the DI indicated I was assisting on the murder case. His reply was that how come we didn't know the Hamilton lot were doing undercover work on our turf. I frantically gestured to the Boss about things, and he had it all sorted. He said he did know about the Undercover team from Hamilton, and it was something to do with drugs and importation. Not our case but he was kept well aware by the Hamilton team about their operation. I have to say that I was impressed with the Boss. He was a very smooth liar! With that the big Boss hung up.

The Boss then said, "When the Papers get hold of something, he always gets his knickers in a wad. He can usually tell when he is going to get a call from them, and he waffles about Police work and the papers say they received 'no Comment' from the Police. It's a fairly standard routine with the Boss and it's also not my problem. I tell you what. It's not far off five o'clock. Let's call it a day and we'll pick this up in the morning."

I'm a starter for an early night so I left with the Boss and went home.

Friday

Always in bright and early I was of course beaten by the Sarge. One of the DCs went across for our coffee and I sat with the Sarge while we waited for the coffee to arrive. The Sarge didn't have much to say so we went into the Boss's office and looked at the whiteboard. Did I mention that the Sarge had purchased his boat and was busy terrorizing the trout on Lake Tarawera. Well he had, and occasionally I would get tales of how long it took to land this fish or how big that fish was that got away. The Sarge was now keeping an eye out for good fishing weather. Today was a warm day so he reckoned he might be out fishing that evening. The Sarge's wife, Huia, reckoned the Sarge should take more notice of the Māori fishing calendar but that was not the Sarge's way of doing things.

Back to the whiteboard. The Sarge and were perusing the board when the coffee came. We sat on the edge of the Boss's desk while we examined the board. The Sarge was ticking off the various points we had mentioned.

"You haven't put up a decent off-road car park. It's well set back from the road. There would have been up to eight cars parked up there. He would need a decent sized section to hold that many motors. It couldn't be worse if you are getting down to the business and someone is knocking on the bedroom door asking you to move your car."

I hadn't thought of that, so I added it to the list. Behind my back the Boss walked in, "Hello you two? Trying my desk on for size, are you?"

We were aware the Boss was only joking so I updated the board and filled the Boss in on what we had done.

The Sarge wandered out to his desk. When he came back with the list of what the CIB needed to attend to, he looked a little concerned. "A couple of more ram raids, last night. That's disappointing. Also a domestic and a commercial burglary. I was having a beer last night with one of the squaddies in the Police Pub. He reckons they're getting an increase in car thefts. Nothing to worry us about yet, but he did say that they were getting almost a car a night. Mainly big dollar vehicles or bigger sized motors. Maybe they are being stolen to order."

Just then the Boss's phone rang, and he answered with his usual, "Hello!"

After a few seconds of conversation the Boss replied, "No, you wait. Me and the DS will come over.

Although I was still finishing my coffee the Boss was impatient. "No DS. You finish your coffee first. It's no matter that we are keeping the Squaddie waiting on his way to the next emergency he has to deal with. You finish your coffee. Oh, you'll finish it on your way over! How civic minded of you!"

Occasionally the Boss is humorously sarcastic. I'm not sure today was one of those days!

With that the Boss was out of the front door and walking across Fenton St. I was scurrying to catch up with him while still drinking my coffee. Well I had paid for it, so I wanted to enjoy it!

When we got over there the Boss was striding out and going upstairs. We went into the Squaddies' room and the Boss was busy bending someone's ear. I was probably a couple of seconds behind, but the Boss made the Squaddie repeat what he was saying.

"Yeah, like I was saying. They're organised. So far, it's happened twice last night and twice the night before. They'll ram raid a place, a dairy of or booze store get in and get out within a couple of minutes and they also have a vehicle parked with a couple of lads down the street. They seem to be timing us from when the alarm goes off. Yeah, we'll search their vehicle but it's always clean and legal. One of them said to me the other night, 'Well done Mr. Policeman. That's a new record. 7 minutes and 27 seconds'. They seem to know how long they have got!"

The Boss replied, "That's what I was worried about. If they are timing your response, they know how long they have got. It sounds similar to what they had in Hamilton. Leave it with me and I'll see what I can do. Come on, Detective Sergeant. You have finished your coffee? Oh, Constable. We're getting reports of stolen cars coming across the road. What do you reckon. Stolen to order? Shipped overseas?"

"Personally I reckon they are getting nicked to do the ram raids. We've had a couple of vehicles last night that turned up on the stolen vehicles list that were used for the ram raid. Usually a bigger motor or something like a Ute with a bit of grunt. But that's only my opinion. I reckon they will need a decent sized motor to get a better access to the dairies. Something with a bit of grunt behind it."

The Boss thanked the Squaddie for bringing it to our attention. I then followed the Boss back over the road to our 'temporary' offices. He got the Sarge in and then spoke, "It seems like this lot are as well organised as the Hamilton lot. It looks like I'll have to get on the phone to Hamilton and see if we can borrow a few of their lads. Last time we were successful in Hamilton because we were on the scene inside two minutes. We reckon we got over half of the mobs doing these raids. If either of you have no suggestions, I'll get on to Hamilton and perhaps Tauranga and see if we can nip this in the bud."

Also set for that morning was the funeral for the murder victim. The Boss wanted to go and attend the funeral. Said it was one way of showing respect for the loss and it was also a good way of keeping an eye out for who attended the event. He reckoned he could usually tell if there was someone shedding crocodile tears. By that, I assumed he was looking for anyone who didn't seem to be genuinely mourning. The Boss called it neural linguistic programming. It sounded a bit uppity to my uneducated ears.

Getting back to the ram raids, neither the Sarge nor I had a better suggestion. It seems like being mob handed was the way to go.

The Boss got onto Hamilton, after the funeral, and received a very good reception. He was well liked when he was over there on secondment. The Boss then got on to Tauranga. They were having a similar problem but the raiders over there didn't seem as well organised as the Rotorua mob. The Boss twisted a few arms and they agreed to come over. I think it was because the Boss promised to return the favour.

It was all set down for Monday night. Our Squaddies were instructed to patrol the suburbs for the weekend. I think the Boss was hoping that the Squaddies' presence would deter the ram raiders. We'll never know if it worked, or if the raiders were too busy getting drunk for the weekend. Oh and there was something of a bonus. Using the APNR (Auto number plate recognition system) the Squaddies apprehended a couple of stolen vehicles that were out and about on Sunday night. They may well have been on their way to do a ram raid, but we'll never really know.

I turned up for the Boss's Saturday shift and I had a wonderfully quiet day. I perused the murder case for an hour or two. Then I found a note from the Boss saying I should organise accommodation for all of the visiting lads from Hamilton and Tauranga.

With Rotorua being a tourist town and half the accommodation filled with homeless, it wasn't easy getting rooms for twenty-seven extra people, but I eventually managed it.

At around 5pm I went home and settled down for the weekend. With so many extras, next week was going to be busy.

Also that weekend was the day for putting the clocks back. I think I have it right. We get an extra hours sleep in.

Chapter 5

M<u>onday</u>
I was in at my usual time on Monday. I don't know what I expected but the extras were not going to be arriving until midafternoon. The Boss came in and was immediately collared to go over and see the big Boss.

When the Boss returned, he was less than happy. He called the Sarge and I into his office and shut the door.

He relayed the gist of the conversation he had with the big Boss. It seems the Boss had a phone call from his opposite number in Hamilton this morning. Said he was just checking if everything was ok for the lads coming over; accommodation and how long did he reckon they would be needed etc. As the Boss knew nothing about it, he said he would get on to it and get back to the DI in Hamilton.

"So when I got to his office, you can imagine the reception I got! Right, then the Boss asked me how I was going to handle the spares coming in. I replied that the DS would be in charge of that."

I was a little stunned, but I hadn't really thought it through, "Thanks Boss, and you were going to tell me, when?"

The Boss replied, "Oh it gets better. Evidently that was the wrong answer I gave. It appears we can't have a DS giving orders to a Detective Inspector. That's sending the wrong message. So I was told to give the murder to the DS to handle and I could then comfortably take on the ram raids. I intimated that there may be a problem with the DS taking on the murder and I mentioned the possible conflict of interest with you having met the victim socially. He was not happy. In fact I'd say he was way short of being happy! It would seem that I have to take charge of this ram raid set up and I also have to take on the murder case as well. He muttered something about why the hell do I need a DS if I am taking everything on myself."

I tried to interject, "But Boss, we both know…"

The Boss continued, "Oh and this day just keeps getting better. The Boss wanted to know how many would be available for a welcome to the marae. It seems that is the least we could do".

I was well disappointed and that was an understatement!

"Never mind, DS. If it keeps the Boss happy, I'll go with it. However, I might have spoiled his day just a little by saying we need to keep the spare lads a bit of a secret if they are to be effective in our mission. Now, Detective Sergeant, as part of my taking charge of this case I'd like you to prepare a list of dairies in our fair town. Then I want you to organise a convenient place for these lads to park up so they can be on the spot within a couple of minutes or less. Right, have I forgotten anything Sarge?"

It seemed the Boss was letting me know that I had caused my Boss to displease the big Boss. It would probably end up as my fault, anyway. If it involved the big Boss it usually ended up as my fault.

"Well other than getting the spare lads organised with room keys, getting the motel owners to not mind if they are a bit late back into their rooms, a place to hold a briefing this afternoon and a word to the lads over the road that they might get a bit busy later in the evening. It may even pay to have an extra lad on duty tonight if we do get busy."

"Thanks, Sarge, but I'm sure the DS has already got all of that planned."

With that he walked back into his office and left us outside. I was about to say something when the Sarge walked off humming 'A policeman's lot is not a happy one." It might be from the Gilbert and Sullivan play 'Iolanthe' and this policeman's lot was very definitely not a happy one! I set to and organised the keys to the motel rooms etc. and also a meeting place for this afternoon.

By midafternoon most of the guys from Hamilton had arrived and also most of the lads from Tauranga. There is quite a camaraderie among the boys in blue, so the first few minutes were spent catching up with old mates. Also, a lot of good friendships were made when everyone went to help out the Hamilton Lads. I didn't really know anyone other than the odd person I had met over the years. At 4pm the Boss took on the centre stage role. He allocated 18 squad cars to be at a certain place after seven pm. Which was when it got dark. Some of the squad cars were two handed and some were only with a driver and the understanding that back up would be available. Given that Rotorua was such a geographically large town, it was the best we could do. Most of the Squaddies were two handed and on the first night, we grabbed two ram raiders and seven lads who were turning over the dairies in question. Learning from the Hamilton experience we had already decided that we would run the operation for two nights and then leave it for two nights. So the spares could go home for a couple of nights and then return to Rotorua in a couple of days.

If anything this made us fairly light for the dayshift so when a call came in for the CIB to be involved, quite often we were the first people on the scene. It happens sometimes.

That night we got a couple of ram raiders in Springfield. They hauled them into the cells and were processed. Also we got a car that we assume had been stolen just for the ram raid. That was a bit of a worrying trend as far as the cops were concerned. It looked like they were stealing bigger engined vehicles to facilitate a good entry into the dairies. It looks like the Squaddie from the other day was correct.

<u>Tuesday</u>

On Tuesday morning I was in at my usual time. It was another nice day and the Sarge and I waited for the coffee to be delivered. Of course it didn't come as the two DCs were sleeping off their late nights work. In the end I went over and saw Annie again. I was supposed to keep things quiet, so I never mentioned anything. Annie saw me and immediately asked if Tim was pulling a sickie. It was too difficult to explain so I just said yes.

On Tuesday afternoon we got the spare lads in again. They were sleeping in the morning or doing a bit of sightseeing. It made our office a little crowded, but we managed fine. The Boss stood up and gave his few words of encouragement. Thanked them for the collars the previous night and reminded them to not have a sleep in the squad cars so they were to be ready to go in a moment. With that he gave them their assignments for the night and let them go and get food.

I didn't have that much to do. With the squad cars being tied up doing the ram raids there was no one to deal with the general crime in our patch. I still had to be in early with the Sarge and I reckon my job was pretty much just hanging around and looking busy.

That night we caught three ram raiders plus a couple of stolen vehicles.

Wednesday

The Boss left me a message on my desk. It seems that three of the raiders caught were Mongrel mob lads and he wanted me to go and have a word with Ronnie, their boss. I usually got on well with Ronnie, so I didn't have any concerns about this.

I rang Ronnie at about 10 30 and told him I was on my way. Most people in his line of activity would be concerned about the Cops showing up. Ronnie just said. 'Fine, I'll put the jug on'.

When I got there the car was pulled back from over the gate and I was allowed to walk right in to Ronnie's workshop.

There must have the best part of two hundred grands worth of bikes in the workshop. And all of them Harley Davidsons. Yes, I couldn't help having a quiet drool at some of the machinery parked up.

"On your own today, Bro?" asked Ronnie. "Not often you come visiting without your lads tagging along."

It somehow reminded me that Ronnie didn't get where he was by being just a good fighter. He was also fairly street smart.

"No, the other lads were busy, so I thought I'd come on my Tod."

Once we were sat down Ronnie asked what my visit was about.

"Well it seemed that three of your lads were picked up last night doing a ram raid on a dairy in Springfield. The Boss is not happy that you are branching out. Wanted me to come and have a chat, as it were, you know check you weren't going out of your usual line of business."

"Sorry, Detective Sarge. Not any of my lads." Ronnie had a fair idea of what his lads got up to.

"Well they're banged up in the nick and spouting off they are members of the Mongrel mob. That's why the Boss wanted me to make contact."

"Describe them?"

"Two young lads one with a beard and wearing a Mob T shirt. One has a mob tattoo on his face just about where a beard would cover it. One older lad, I'm gonna say around 25? Big lad. Running a bit to fat rather than a just a big lad."

"Detective Sarge. Can I give them a visit. I think I know who you mean, and my being there will give them a scare. Will they get bail?"

"Dunno. They won't be in court until this afternoon so I can't see why you can't visit with them."

Well Ronnie was already on his feet and striding towards one of the bikes, swinging a leg over he hit the ignition key. I sat back and waited for the initial engine noise to die down and pointed to my head. Ronnie, with a look of resignation on his face got off the Hog and put a helmet on. Then he powered up outside and waited for me to get to my car. Very sedately we went back into town and parked outside the new Copshop.

I used my influence to get Ronnie straight down to the holding cells so he could complete his visit.

When Ronnie saw who was there, he went quiet.

"Detective Sergeant, it might be better if you stay out of the cell while I have a word with my lads."

The constable on duty let Ronnie into the cell. I stood back perhaps ten feet away but still close enough to hear what was being said.

Ronnie let rip into these three. As far as I can tell the older one was a patched member of the gang and the two younger ones were novices or prospects, Ronnie ripped into them about respecting the patch and only doing what they were told they could do.

The older one reckoned it was the younger ones' idea, but Ronnie wasn't having any of that!

At one point Ronnie clouted one of the younger ones across the head and the constable in charge of the cells moved forward. I held one hand up and said to Ronnie, "Ronnie, we're not supposed to beat up the prisoners in the cells. I reckon this constable thinks that should also apply to you."

Ronnie was not really contrite, but he did say, "Sorry about that, Sarge. I'll give them a good talking to when we get back to the site, if that's okay with the constable, there."

Ronnie spent just a few more minutes in the cell and then he came out and spoke to me. The constable was trying hard not to make out he was also listening.

"Sorry about that Detective Sarge. Butch is easily led, and the young lads were saying how easy it would be. He may be a good lad in a scrap and he's a bloody wizard with engines, But..."

I couldn't help it. I had to add "But....?"

"Nah, thick as two short planks. What will happen to these idiots?"

"Probably they will get bail and then reappear for a court date. But bail isn't guaranteed. After that they might get time depending on their records and if they keep their mouth shut about being involved in the Mongrel Mob."

"Serves them right. You tell your Boss the Mob won't be taking part in any more of these ram raids. OK? If there's nothing else, I'll bugger off back to View Road and make sure these lads are made welcome when they get back."

Ronnie and I shook hands and he left. It's an odd code that these gang members live under. They have to respect the patch and do what they are told. I've heard a few things about their initiation, and I can only say that you have to want to be in a gang in New Zealand.

By the time I got back across the road, the Boss was in and quite chipper. He was happy with the success of the two previous nights. I filled him in with what had gone on between Ronnie and his lads. The Boss was even more merry with that and reminded me I should be prepared to say a few words about that, the next time the lads are down from Hamilton and Tauranga. He reckoned it would cheer them up no end.

The two Dc's were tidying up paperwork from the previous two nights' work. The Sarge was busy attending to the counter, and I was busy making my lunch. The spare lads were not due until Friday for the Friday and Saturday nights efforts, so the Boss suggested I take the rest of the day off. With me doing the Boss's shift on Saturday it felt like I was working twenty-four /seven, so I was quite happy. I actually took lunch back to my place and had a lazy day on the couch where I dozed off watching the golf. Maybe I if actually took up golf I might be more interested. It's something I must have thought of as I dozed. When I woke up, I took a long look at being a golfer on You Tube. Yes, it looked complicated but surely not for a hacker like me. Note I am already using the right term for an amateur golfer. A hacker!

<u>Thursday.</u>

As usual, I was in bright and early and went over for the coffee for me and the Sarge. It had turned a bit murky and I hadn't put my coat in my motor so I got a bit wet walking over to the coffee shop. Annie asked me if I was ordering the two DCs, but I didn't know so I just said no.

On going back to the Sarge with his coffee I went over the items that needed CIB input. There was only one ram raid, so that was a plus, a couple of burglaries and an assault that we should look at. A fairly busy Wednesday night for Rotorua. I allocated the two DCs to the burglaries and I handled the assault. Some guy mouthing off at a pub and someone had taken offense. I had the two parties in separate cells as the mouthy guy had been arrested for being drunk and disorderly when the Squaddies arrived.

It was one of those times when I was happy the new Copshop had more than one interview room. The mouthy guy had been spouting off some fairly direct comments about Asian Immigrants. Obviously, he had a few under his belt. As far as I can make out there were a few of the lads in the pub who were ready to 'quieten' this guy down when one guy hauled off and dropped him. I knew that it would have to be a situation where the Police would be the only ones that would press charges. My job was to decide whether the Police wanted to put the time of the court in this.

As I was busy with the Hamilton lads coming over, I figured it was easier to let this one go.

I interviewed both parties, but I may have laid an undue influence on about the racist remarks and anyone in the pub could have chosen to lay a racial discrimination charge against this guy. He was already barred from going to the pub again. In the end I let them both off with a caution and a stern admonition to the guy making the racist remarks.

Releasing the pair of them I walked back over to our office. The Boss was having a day off, I discovered, and he would be back in again on Friday. Tim Cross also approached me to remind me that I would have to cover his shift on Saturday as he would be going out with the spare lads from Tauranga. My day was just getting better and better. I was at the stage of just assuming I would be covering the Saturday shift anyway.

After lunch I had a visitor. It was Robin Nicholson, said he had just dropped in to check up on any progress we had made with the case that he could perhaps relate back to the widow. When he saw me, he looked just a little disappointed. Perhaps he wondered If he had made an impolite remark to my bird when we were sat at the table. I didn't give him the satisfaction of knowing Janet wouldn't have gone upstairs with any of these, what did she call them? That's right, she called them Tossers.

Any way as far as Robin was concerned, I could only add that the widow was being kept appraised of any progress and if he needed more info than that he should talk to the DI who was taking the lead in the case.

I updated the Sarge on the day's events. He agreed that the Mongrel Mob did not take kindly to anyone who disrespected their patch. He reckoned he would not care to be in the shoes of the lads over the road when they did get back to the Gang HQ.

I spent the next hour or so working on the murder case. I came up with nothing, but I was impressed with the Boss's working out of who bonked who at the party on the Friday night. Very convoluted and, it appears, they were a very friendly bunch of people!

Friday

Another murky day. I was in at my usual time and as usual the Sarge beat me in again. He picked up the notes from over the road. The ones where the CIB should get involved and he passed them across to me.

I was wondering where the two DC's were when it occurred to me that they would be coming in later. So the net result was that I would be handling all of the cases today. How wonderful!

Looking at what I had to handle, I remarked that the criminal fraternity in our fair city were keeping to their usual routine of being busy on a Thursday night. One domestic assault, always the priority, one GBH, probably drinking was involved, and the offender was over the road in the cells, and a couple of commercial burglary cases.

Once I had my coffee, I made a start on the day. The domestic assault always took first priority. In Hillcrest the neighbor had gone off at their neighbor for blasting loud music until after midnight. The Squad car had deemed it as a 50/50 incident and let both of them off with a warning. I still had to attend so I made my way up there. Both of the neighbours were home, so we all sat down and had a cup of tea around the dining table. The net result was that we all agreed it would be better if the first neighbor kept the noise down after 10.30 at night and the second neighbor agreed it might be better if she made a phone call first instead of banging on the neighbor's ranch slider at some time after midnight. I reckon I brokered the peace, but it would not surprise me if it became a regular 'incident' address. We do have a few of them where we know that we will need some assistance.

My GBH case had already been handled in court. It appears the assailant was well oiled and had smacked a fellow patron who had been quietly drinking at the bar. The assailant was still under the weather when he appeared before the Judge. He had been stood down and would reappear in the afternoon when he was hopefully a bit more sober. I did pop in and interview the assailant and I also popped into the pub where he had been drinking. He'll probably get a fine and a breach of the peace order and also be banned for six months from the pub. Out of all of the punishments I think the ban from the pub will be the most effective deterrent.

It was already past 11.00 when I turned up to the commercial burglary and they were both on the same street! The first one looked like an inside job. Obviously, a key had been used on the rear door. I was reluctant to tell the owner he had a tea leaf on his staff. That's a thief, if you're wondering. But I did manage to summon up the right phrases, and suggest that he might first look at anyone who had a grievance against him, Staff member etc.

Oddly enough, I had the same situation up the road. Looked like an inside job. Obviously, a key holder had used his or her key in an out of hours capacity. You do have to be careful in these situations. You can't offend anyone nowadays. I said all the usual platitudes and disappeared. Most of the damage and losses would be covered by insurance, anyway. I gave them an incident number to report to their insurance and left it at that.

By the time I got back to the nick it was a little before 1.00 so I had my lunch and was busy reading the papers online when the Boss walked in being his usual chipper self.

"Hello to all of the wage slaves," he said.

The Sarge replied that obviously the Boss was doing it for the love of the job. That was well received so the Boss asked how I had got on with being a real detective this morning. As in he knew full well that anything that came in this morning would have to be handled by my own self.

"Yeah, thanks for that, Boss. A domestic in Hillcrest which ended up with everyone being polite. I've marked it in the incident book so if we get another call, we'll know to take support. A GBH which will be handled in the court this afternoon. The guy was still unfit to plead when he first appeared, and the Judge held him until this afternoon so he might sober up. A couple of commercial burglaries that look like an inside job. No sign of forced entry. Thief knew what they were after, and the investigations were all over and done with by lunch. Well, a late lunch anyway. By the sound of it you're well rested and looking forward to tonight."

"Yeah, looking forward to tonight. If we get the same number of cars out tonight, we should have the town covered. I assume Tim told you about you covering his shift on Saturday?"

"Yeah. Really glad to be of service!" If that sounded just a bit sarcastic, it did manage to convey my feelings.

The Boss mentioned that I'd better not forget I had to say a word on the Mob's involvement and what Ronnie had said. Oh, this day just keeps getting better!

By midafternoon the spare lads were piling into the office over the road from the new copshop. All of them thought it was a brilliant idea to have the CIB away from the workings of the big Boss. It must have been around four in the afternoon that the Boss called everyone together to give them a pep talk for the evening and he also got me up to say a few words on how Ronnie had reacted to finding out about his prospects getting involved with the ram raids. My few words got good laughs, so I found myself being involved on the fringe of the organising for the evening's activities.

A little after 5.00 I went home and had a quiet evening. No doubt I'd have a busy day if Rotorua was subject to its usual Friday nighttime activity.

Chapter 6

Saturday

I was in at my usual time on Saturday. I went and grabbed a coffee and with that in hand I entered the office. Friday night had been another success. Another two ram raiders locked up. Although they had no obvious affiliations with criminal gangs it was still good to get these lads tidied away. I say lads but one of the raiders had a girl in their ranks. This was a surprise for the Squaddies as they suddenly had to find a WPC to do a search on this girl. And this girl definitely knew her rights as far as that was concerned. I believe they called in a WPC from home. By the time she got her uniform on and her lipstick on straight she was probably up for three hours of overtime. The last thing you want in this type of case is someone doing you for sexual harassment.

For me, I had a light day - a domestic burglary and a couple of domestic assaults. There was also a ram raid, but we were told to leave that side of life to the DCs. I'm surprised the spares had not caught the guy but it was out past the airport, so we were not as well covered out that far. Reading the Squaddies' report I had both of the assaults down as someone having had too much booze. Yes, we still had to attend but it's amazing how many things get glossed over in the cold light of day. When you are inebriated, everything seems important but when the cold light of day hits you, suddenly it doesn't seem quite so important.

I attended both domestic assaults. Neither victim wanted it to go any further. Surprisingly one of the victims was a male. His wife had come from the pub and let loose on him. Not really my problem if they won't press charges. I urged all parties to go up to the hospital to get checked over although I'll assume neither of them did.

The domestic burglary was something different, for a change. The couple had gone away for the night to see rellies in Taupo or wherever. They had mentioned it in the neighborhood but didn't think any more about it. When they got back early in the morning, they discovered they had been burgled. Putting two and two together, I walked around the immediate neighborhood and soon came across a likely candidate. Let's say this person was fairly well known to us. The Squaddies were called, and a search warrant was executed. We found all of the missing items in this guy's house. Funny, it was easier for a Judge to sign a search warrant than it was to get a squad car on that particular morning. Anyway, the homeowner was more than happy to press charges so that resulted in an arrest and the burglar being held over for the weekend. Other than it gave me a bit of paperwork to do, I was quite pleased that I had a result!

It almost seems that a lot of our work is settling domestic or neighbours disputes. Sometimes it can get a little frustrating.

It might have been heading for 3.00 when the Boss came in. Once he started the ball kept rolling as more and more of the 'spare lads" wandered in and made themselves a brew. The coffee shop at the library closed around 1pm on a Saturday so they had to make do with a brew.

The Boss gave them all their orders. They left around 4.00 to get some food for the evening. That left the Boss and I to sit and chat.

"It's all going well!" I added to the conversation.

"Yeah." the Boss agreed but he was disappointed that they hadn't got any of the big players yet. There was usually someone at the top who was ready to take the fags off the small players hands. There was a ready market in Auckland. Perhaps that's why they called it the 'Big Smoke'.

The Boss was still happy that we had caught a few in our net, and during our conversation he wondered whether it was worth keeping the 'spare lads' coming down. I was quite happy either way. Anyway, the Boss decided not to made a decision to get the spares coming down until next Friday. That meant I would have the added benefit of the two DCs for the week ahead. That is until the Boss reminded me that I would also have to cover Dave's shift the following Saturday as he would be busy with the 'spare lads'.

Tomorrow will be my day off. Boy, am I looking forward to it.

At 5.00 I left the Boss holding the fort and I went home to enjoy my one day off.

Sunday

During the Sunday, I decided to go up to the Springfield Golf course to have a look at what golfers do. I went to Springfield place because the big Boss was already a member at the Whaka Golf club, or to give it it's full name of 'Arikikapapa', and I didn't want to run the risk of bumping into him.

I did have a word with the pro. He assessed me as being reasonably fit. A walk around a golf course would not be a problem for me. He also mentioned he had a secondhand set of clubs for perhaps $500 that would do me for a while. Looking in his book he noted he had an hour free on Tuesday. Plenty of time for a lesson and he would not charge me for the lesson if I purchased the clubs from him. It was not the time to ring the Boss, so I decided to leave it until Monday. Promising to get back to the Club pro I left with my new set of clubs and decided to have a look on You tube. Surely this golf thing wasn't that hard. I mean I'd seen fairly unfit lads having a go and they were giving it heaps.

Looking at the videos on YouTube may have given me a false sense of security, I suck at golf!

Monday

In at my usual time. Still my turn to go and get the coffee. Evidently Annie plays the odd game of golf. Maybe one day I could play a round with her?

On Saturday night they had caught one more ram raider. The 'spares' were happy when the Boss said he'd like to leave it until next Friday. It made little difference to them, but they might be able to get the wife and kids over to Rotorua for a weekend on the Forces expenses. We don't get that many perks, so a win is a win!

I mentioned to the Boss that I had purchased some golf clubs and I mentioned that on Tuesday the Pro had a spare hour. The Boss firstly looked at me as if I was mad. Then he suggested it could be a great idea and why did I not think of this before. Just what I needed to keep myself occupied. I could never really tell when he was being sarcastic, so I said thanks and rang the Pro to book the time.

I had the two DCs otherwise occupied so I took on the case load from over the road. It was one of those nights where everyone in town behaved themselves, it rarely happens so I enjoy it when I can. There was only one case to deal with. A case of GBH at the Palace Tavern. It was easier to walk up to the Palace so that is what I did. I had a look at the security footage, and it was readily apparent what had happened. Someone with too many drinks under their belt had a go at a fellow patron.

Unfortunately the drunk was one of those mean drunks that don't know when to stop. The long and the short of it was that the innocent party, (we assume he was innocent) ended up in the A&E ward and later was transferred to the surgical ward for corrective surgery. The drunk was calmed down but when the Squaddies arrived, he took it personally. He had a go at them but that was about all he managed. The Squaddies are trained in unarmed combat and also in the best use of their baton. If I was the slightest bit interested in the fracas, I might possibly have said that one of the Squaddies might have used their baton with a little more force than usual. Suffice it to say that the assailant was subdued and would be appearing in court later that day. Given the severity of the beating he inflicted on the other guy, I can't see this guy getting out anytime soon.

The Sarge handed me the reports from over the road, the ones that required CIB input. There was nothing that was urgent, but I was happy to hand them over to the DCs. That's when the Boss told me he had given the DCs the day off, so it was still down to me to handle anything. Excellent!

I was looking through the list and making a sort of priority order. There really was nothing that warranted urgent action, so I spent a few more minutes talking about the weekend's activities with the Sarge and the Boss.

At 10.30 the Boss was called over for an urgent meeting with the CI. The Sarge commented that this didn't sound that positive.

When the Boss returned, he filled us in on what the big Boss had said. I have to say that it must have been a slow news day for the local rag, so they had grabbed anything to make a headline. The headline read something like "Rotorua ram raiders. Dairies say they have had enough!"

The paper went into the details of what ram raids had happened and where, and then it interviewed a few dairy owners. There was just a hint of vigilante vengeance, but it must have focused on the lack of police action in bringing these miscreants to justice. Obviously, the big Boss had been asked for comment and he had promised to get back to the papers with a comment. He asked the Boss what they were doing about it. I can imagine full well how the conversation would have gone. A fairly loud and self-exculpating session followed by a quieted down and mainly pissed off explanation.

The Boss had explained what the spare lads were doing and mentioned that they were not coming down until Friday. That obviously did not please the big Boss until the Boss explained it was of no use to have it happen every day. Unless the big Boss wanted the ram raiders to simply wait for the spare lads to go home and then resume their activities. When the big Boss asked what he was to say to the newspapers, it can't have helped that my Boss simply said, "Not my problem, and you can't say anything about the Spare lads either."

With that parting shot the Boss had walked out of the big Boss's office. I'd be tempted to put that one down as a win for my Boss!

My meagre case list had me looking at a domestic assault where the victim had been already assaulted a number of times. It was down to me to make a call where I had to decide if the Police wanted to pursue the case from the Police standpoint. In some cases the Police can make the charges if the witness guarantees they will stand and testify. I'd discuss this with the Boss and then make the decision.

I also had a couple of domestic burglaries where I ended up calling the fingerprint lads in. Other than that I'd compare prints to our existing database or wait until someone matching the prints turned up and we'd have them for a string of offenses.

Going back to the station, I was in a pensive mood. The Sarge had recently made Senior Sergeant and I had only a year less service than him. It might have been two years. Maybe it was time I did the Senior Sergeants exam? By the time I got back to our little office I had decided I should do it. That along with the golf would give me a new reason to, what... Strive? Yes, that would be my new year's resolution even though it was halfway through April.

The Sarge and the Boss were in deep conversation when I returned. They were sat in the Boss's office and when the Boss saw me, he called me in to join them.

The Boss recapped their discussion, "We're getting reports that the dairies are getting organised. Firstly they are busy contacting builders to see if they can get those concreted barrier things put in front of their door. Secondly, they are talking about getting organised with baseball bats and the like. God help us if someone mentions a gun or something. Next, they reckon we should be doing more to help them run their business. Somehow, we should be able to anticipate where these lads are going to hit next and be there mob handed to arrest them."

The Sarge interrupted," I was just saying that we can't tell them about the lads coming over from Hamilton and Tauranga."

The Boss continued, "No, that would give them the heads up. I'd say we have to take this on the chin. Wait till the Daily Ghost hear about the crims we have collared and let them see we are making some inroads."

"How are the dairies doing for getting the builders set up?" I asked.

The Boss replied, "They're doing fine other than getting these barriers, the concrete ones. Seems like there's a national shortage of them due to the demand, and it's right across the country. Every place is getting hammered by these ram raiders. Cheap smokes are big business everywhere. Firths have their lads on overtime to try and keep up with the demand. Serves the government right for pushing the prices of smokes so high. What did they expect would happen. Everyone would give up smoking. Yeah. Right!"

I had my turn, "So, you've had a word with the big Boss that he can't mention the spare lads, and when do we start getting these lads through the courts. These ram raiders?"

"I think the first case is up for trial tomorrow," said the Sarge. "Tomorrow we'll find out if the Courts are going to be hard on them or just give them a slap on the wrist. "

The Boss had his input, "Well the CP is going to try for being hard on them. He has a whole load of dairy owners willing to testify about the hardship this has caused. Let's hope we don't get a judge that wants to stop everyone having a fag. That would be all we need!"

With that the conversation ended. I went and had my lunch and then looked around for something to do. I wandered into the Boss's office and sat down. We discussed the murder case for a while and then the conversation shifted to whether or not the Boss should take up golf. Part of me wanted the Boss to take it up and a part of me didn't. I reckon it was the part that was scared I'd suck at golf and that I didn't want the Boss to be a witness to my humiliation.

Whatever the case, I had my first lesson booked in for tomorrow morning at ten.

<u>Tuesday</u>

I was bright and early for the lesson. The Boss had told me to take the morning off and he would handle the cases from over the road. That meant he would probably hand most of the work over to the two DCs, but it was not my problem.

I had a golf lesson to deal with or learn from.

I do like Springfield as a course. I was busy getting my putter working on the practice green when the Pro called me over.

Using a cart we went over to the practice fairways where he set me up. Firstly he explained the role of the various clubs. Some went high and short. Some went long and low. Given that I already understood that much from You Tube I was well ready for a whack at a ball.

He let me have five whacks at a golf ball with the two wood. They were all over the place. He said nothing to me, just indicated I should go again.

Having hit five he stopped me and explained what I was doing wrong. My right shoulder was weaker than my left shoulder. Probably because I wrote with my right hand. He corrected or adjusted my grip. He reckoned it was easier to teach a middle-aged bloke to work with what they have rather than to make sure he was doing everything in the correct manner. He then walked twenty yards down the fairway and asked me to send a ball only as far as him. I should add that I was to use the two wood. That wasn't too hard. Then he walked another twenty yards and asked for the same. Easy!

Then another twenty yards and so on until I was hitting a ball the best part of 150 yards and fairly straight down the middle.

Then he asked me to change the club for a five iron. Same thing, twenty yards and then another twenty etc. He worked me through the clubs until I was doing a reasonable job with all of the clubs and said I was a natural right hander with a tendency to hook the ball. I assumed that was reasonable, so I took that as a plus. Well pleased with my lesson I went into the office. That's when it hit the fan!

The morning local paper had come out and the big Boss had mentioned that we were having to get people from out-of-town police forces to help deal with our problems! There was an inference about other forces (I don't know, Defence forces?) also being used in a similar manner to when the Covid hit us. The Boss and the Sarge were.... can I say disappointed with the comment? Disappointed would not cover the Boss and the Sarge's moods.

The Boss and the big Boss had already had a few words. If you read that correctly, the Boss had gone over to the big Boss's office, and they had a shouting match. It seems the big Boss had only said that about the spare lads being used in an 'off the record' remark. It was all down to who said what, but the Boss and the big Boss were shouting at each other. The Boss had to make a call about whether the spare lads were to be called for this weekend. It all got quite messy. Possibly to divert attention the big Boss had not so tactfully enquired how the murder investigation was going. That only resulted in another shouting match! All in all, it was probably just as well that I had been away for the morning!

Once things had calmed down sufficiently for reason to prevail, we had a talk and the Boss decided to go ahead with this weekends out of towners being called in. The Sarge reluctantly agreed so we were still set for the weekend.

It was Sarge who asked how my golf lesson had gone on. Surprisingly, the Boss was also interested. I could happily announce that the Pro had called me a natural right hander. Ok, so I left out the bit about having a tendency to hook the ball, and I had been invited to go out with the Pro on Thursday. They had a group of three Pros who went out on a Thursday, and I would make up the fourth. According to the Pro it would be good if I saw how the Pros went and it could be a project for all three Pros to give me a tip or two. Obviously, it was a no because of what the big Boss had done. Surprisingly the Boss said I should go. I had to cover Dave's Saturday shift and I was due for a day off. So why not? Before the Boss could change his mind, I was on the phone, and it was all set up. I should be there before 9.00 on Thursday and it would be on the house.

So I was in a good mood when I got down to work. There had been another couple of commercial burglaries that the Boss had handed on to the two DCs. Both had been inside jobs so the two DCs made the correct platitudes and left it with the business owner.

The Boss handled a case of GBH, and the assailant was known to us. The Boss arrested the guy, and he was held in the cells until he could face a bail hearing in the morning.

The Boss had made very little progress with the murder case. I'm not surprised as the ram raiders were taking up a lot of his time but the big Boss's digging this morning had made my Boss revisit the case. He had contacted the widow, and she was happy that my Boss was still on to it. I think she believed that one of the guests at their party was possibly a suspect and didn't want to think her hubby may have been topped by one of their guests. Possibly someone she herself had been bonking.

With that the day petered out and I left just after 5.00 to go and have a quiet evening. Okay, I probably watched a few videos on You Tube about golf. After all I was out with the Pros on Thursday!

Wednesday

I was just a bit later in than my usual time. I had a twitchy right shoulder. A bit difficult to have a shower, but nothing major. I handed out the cases to the two DCs and I ended up with one. A domestic burglary in Lynmore. When I rolled up to the address my initial thoughts were that it was an inside job, but I soon let that idea go once I had perused the scene. This was a very professional job. Okay, they smashed the downstairs window but they had taped over it first so the glass would not shatter. The people had been home asleep, and the burglary did not wake them up, although they claimed they were light sleepers. I'd read the reports on sleep patterns. When you are deep asleep there is not a lot that can wake you. Something to do with REM or something like that.

Cash and jewelry gone. Small appliances gone. A nice painting gone. A few nice silver frames gone along with their photos. The job would have been over and done with within five minutes. To me it looked like a professional job, but I still had to get the fingerprint lads in and a photographer. Then there was writing a report, an incident number for the insurance and whole host of little bits and pieces. Really this was what I joined the CIB for. Not the myriad little domestics where no one wanted to press charges.

Going back to our office I was just a little pleased that I had a real sort of crime to deal with. I prepared a case file and did my write up and report. I phoned the victim and gave them the incident number. It almost felt pleasant to be working on a proper crime. I'm not forgetting the murder, it's just not my case, really.

I was waiting for the photos and prints to come in so I could really do a job on this case. The other two, the DCs were already back in the office. They had a couple of commercial burglaries. Well, one was retail, and one was commercial. Oddly enough with today's virtually cashless society we seldom get a break in where the loose cash is the target. There are so few people paying in cash today that we find it's not worth the bother of a break-in. Nowadays we find the break ins are more connected to small appliance stores where the gear can be flicked off in the pub or the new trend is using Trade me to flick off nicked items.

Back to the DCs. The retail looked like an inside job and the commercial was for tools and stuff lying around. I sympathize with mechanics because you might spend twenty years building up a decent toolkit and then it's gone over night.

The retail burglary was a coincidence. Very seldom you will get three inside jobs in a row, but I guess it must happen.

I had call from Ronnie, the head of the Mongrel Mob. One of the two younger lads had decided he no longer wished to join the Mob. The other one had taken his punishment as had the patched member. But the first one had declined so he was now out of the Mob. I think the reason Ronnie rang was that he wanted to keep the relationship he had with the Cops on a fairly civil level. The Boss agreed and reckoned he thought better of Ronnie as a result of his call.

The Boss quizzed me about how my golf was going, not that I had had an actual game yet. It seems that the Boss was seriously thinking about taking up golf. I reckoned I could get a good deal for him from the Club Pro, so he said he would think a bit more about it. Said he'd check with the Missus if she didn't mind.

I left a little after 5.00 and went home. I was looking to get a good night's sleep in before my game with the professionals. Yes, I did look at a few more videos on You Tube before settling down for an early night.

Thursday

I was up bright and early for my game. Probably a little too early as I had to have an extra coffee before the game. Ok, so I am keen!

Going out to Springfield I was a mix of nervousness and happiness. Nervous that I might stuff up but happy I would have three Pros who could give me advice. First, I had a session on the practice greens. Evidently that is where the big scores come from. If I can get the hang of putting, everything else will fall into place.

The first thing the Pro did was tell me off!

He reckoned I hadn't cleaned my clubs since I had the lesson with him a couple of days ago. He walked back into his shop and walked out again with a small towel. "Your clubs are important. Keep them clean." A bit curt I thought but he is the expert.

At the first tee I was second to tee off. The first Pro put it down the middle of the fairway. My first ball went close to the fifth tee, but we managed to find it. The other two Pros both put their balls down the middle of the fairway. So I was the next to play. I found the fairway and then lost it again as my ball went down the eighteenth. Still me to play, by good fortune I found the green. Now, surely my practice on the practice greens would pay off. Okay, I made a three putt and everyone else holed out for a birdie. The second at Springfield is a big drop down to the hole. Again I shot well left of the hole by around forty yards. My fellow players were all on the green with their first shot. Perhaps I took a six or a seven. After that we were on to the long holes. This is where I really let fly and really stuffed up.

On the fourth hole I finally got the advice I wanted, "Only swing with 60% of your effort. Then build it up to no more than 80%."

Well I did try, and the day got better. After a while my fellow players realised, they could have a joke with me. From seemingly impossible instructions that I was physically incapable of doing, they relented, and I actually enjoyed my game with them. I probably hit somewhere the wrong side of 120 shots, but I was getting just a little more consistent by the time I finished. For my first game, I was happy and probably hooked! More importantly, the fellow Professionals were not afraid to give me tips on how to play better.

Going back to my place for a quick shower I was into the office by 1.00. The Boss was interested in how I had got on, as was the Sarge. When I told them how it had actually gone, they seemed pleased. Getting back to being a detective was my next job. So I asked how things had gone this morning. A quiet sort of day was how the Boss described it. A couple of GBH cases and a domestic burglary were about it.

The Sarge had nothing to really occupy him, so we met in the Boss's office and chewed the fat with the Boss.

I think everyone was concerned about the effect on the weekend that the big Boss's faux pas may have, but we agreed there was sod all we could do about it. The murder case was discussed with nothing being resolved. Oh, and Robin Nicholson had called in again enquiring if we had any news to report back to the widow? I briefly wondered if he was doing a bit on the side with the widow, but I was too polite to mention it to the Boss. If the Boss had the same thought, he was keeping it quiet.

Oh and the Boss had to remind me that I should be doing something about accommodation for the 'spare lads.' Last Friday the Sarge had organised it all and it was not a job he wanted to deal with again. That sent me on a hunt for accommodation all around town. I did get it sorted but it wasn't easy to do at the last minute. A few of the lads received an upgrade in their accommodation thanks to it being such short notice. I'm afraid I was too happy to get the accommodation and less concerned with which ranks got the better motels!

Friday

On the Friday I was in at my usual time and was sent by the Sarge to get the coffee as the two DCs were working late that day. While sitting and enjoying our coffee the Boss walked in and joined us. It seems he had forgotten about being on late duty and had come in at his normal time. We talked about the murder case and also what was going on with the ram raiders' cases. The courts had already dealt with some of the cases and the usual term was one month to three months inside if we could get the offender to admit he was a repeat offender. Sometimes a driving license was suspended but, if nothing else, we were getting them off the street. The Boss reckoned we were missing something, but it was just a hunch on his part. He left the office and went home for a lie in, and the Sarge and I dealt with the crimes requiring CIB input. I received a call from the police psychologist. He had been looking at all the cases and my case of someone spraying weedkiller on local sports grounds was 'interesting.' and he just wanted to touch base with me as I was the main guy on the case. He really went over stuff we had talked about before.

He reckoned I could be up for problems from the mystery weedkiller. After the first case he had received quite a bit of coverage in the local paper but he had not gotten a mention with the next two cases. Usually this type of offender reveled in the publicity he received.

Having received no publicity, the psychologist reckoned he may try something where he did get publicity. He reckoned a good arson always got local publicity and maybe even national publicity as well. There was always a chance that the spraying guy may not try anything else if he was satisfied but he did say I should be prepared for anything further up the scale.

He was a good guy, the psychologist, and I chatted with him for a further ten minutes. Among the things he recommended was that if it was taken to the next level one of the firefighters should take a video of the crowd gathered, and there would be a crowd. There was always a crowd at an arson scene and that could be a good way to spot the guy. I thanked him for his time and the call and he said it was fine, glad to be of any help, that's what he was paid for, to see if he could advise local officers what to look for. When he rang off I got on the phone to the fire brigade lads. I told them about my call with the psychologist and his suggestion that my weed killer guy may up his game. The local fire brigade usually had one guy assigned to videoing the crowds and how the brigade fought the fire etc. I was glad I made the call and expanded on my circle of contacts.

It was a fairly quiet day, one domestic and one burglary, commercial.

I attended the domestic first. There was no assault but there had been a lot of screaming and shouting at a time after midnight. Turns out our hubby had been out late and when he got home wifey didn't give him as warm a reception as he had expected. Wifey reckoned he had been with a woman. He'd come home feeling just a touch randy. Not a good mix! The neighbours had called it in because the noise was waking up their kids. Again, it's something of a marriage guidance thing for me and to stay in the middle of them so they don't harm each other. It's just another one of those disturbances where neither will get down to pressing charges against each other. It filled in an hour but it was mostly a waste of my time.

The commercial burglary was worthwhile. Forced entry on the rear door. No Alarm. Cash taken and a few brand-new tools. It might be worth a visit to the local bars to see if anyone was trying to flog cheap tools. I got the fingerprint lads down and I took a few photos. The owner was on the blower trying to get an alarm system installed. As everyone he rang was met with the same incredulous "How Much?" I didn't think the owner would learn much from this lesson. It's not my problem but I would recommend every business owner to have a half decent alarm system fitted. Even the sticker on the wall outside could be a deterrent. Oh Just one thing. There are also any number of false alarm systems on the market for a couple of hundred dollars. They might show an alarm outside, but it isn't actually connected to anything! The real professionals recognised these brands and they're not worth the effort of screwing them to the wall. Get a decent alarm fitted! Most insurance companies will give a discount if you have a decent alarm system.

I left the scene of the commercial burglary and went back to our nick.

The Sarge was in on his own. As we had nothing to do with regard to paperwork, I let the Sarge regale me about the latest one that got away. I asked what he was doing with all of these fish that he caught. Surely his missus was getting over the prospect of having fresh fish on the table every night. He reckoned it was the sheer joy of catching and releasing them that was the buzz. That told me that his missus, Huia, had had enough of trout on the menu most nights.

The fingerprint lads were back from the commercial burglary and had loaded the prints up onto our system. I ran the prints through our system but came up with no matches. Adding the case file to the host of other unsolved crimes I sat back and waited for the' spare lads' to arrive.

At 3.00 they started to arrive, and I greeted them as I now knew most of them by name. The Boss walked in and the two DCs. I made myself appear busy when the phone rang. It was Alain from the place around the back of Hamurana. He was idly wondering about how much progress we had made on the murder case. The Boss suggested he speak to his Boss, Lesley. When Alain inferred that Lesley was away in 'Herbay' the boss took a bit more interest. He wanted to speak to Alain again and this seemed like a good opportunity. Not just at this time!

Alain suggested the Boss (and I) could call out for a coffee at his place on the Monday morning. The lady of the house would not be back until Tuesday. If the Boss promised to ring him when we were about to leave, he would make some fresh baguettes. They would be the real French baguettes and not the cardboard things they served at the local bakery.

Other than the fact that the Boss would have to find out what the heck baguettes were, he now had an appointment on Monday morning. Then it dawned on him that Monday was supposed to be his day off from working on the weekend. Never mind, he would take Tuesday off, instead.

That weekend was something of a non-event for the spare lads. They did get one on the Friday night and one on the Saturday night, but felt they were only local lads having a go at what seemed to be an easy few dollars or, in the second case, a cheap way to get fags for their smoking habit.

The Boss did the interviews on the Saturday and the Sunday, and it confirmed his suspicions. It seemed that the local organised crims were taking note of the spare lads being in town and having the night off. Maybe they were getting the info from the motels with their contacts? In any case the Boss decided to call it a day for the spare lads coming into town for a while.

On the Sunday night, when the spare lads had gone back home, there were three ram raids across the city, and no one was available to deal with them. More and more dairies were getting fitted out with the reinforced concrete posts across their front doors, but it was still relatively easy to drive around and find a dairy without the protection of the concrete posts.

Chapter 7

<u>Monday</u>

In bright and early on Monday I was surprised to see the two DCs in as well. I'd have expected them to take Monday as a day off in lieu for working on the weekend.

According to the two DCs I was expected to go with the Boss out to Alain's place, so the two DC's were to take on the CIB cases. I personally reckon that the Boss was just a little homophobic about a visit to Alain, but I did have the good sense not to mention it to him.

I took the three cases requiring CIB input and handed them out to the DCs, which left the Boss and I to head out to Alain's. The Boss had indeed tried out the baguettes from the local bakery and wondered what the fuss was about. I have to admit I had also tried them and was actually looking forward to trying Alain's baguettes.

On the way out to Alain's, after we had made a phone call to him, the Boss was wondering if we should try a different approach to the murder case. As far as he was concerned, we had been looking for any signs of suspicion among the party enthusiasts with little success and maybe the case was going cold. Maybe we should be looking at just those blokes who had been a bit friendly with each other, in that way, and see if we could get an idea of jealousy among the guys?

I didn't really feel it was my case, so I readily agreed with the Boss.

When we got out to Alain's place we were given instructions on how to enter Alain's flat. He had a good sized flat over the garage, a six-vehicle garage, so he had had a good view of the party unfolding before his uninvited eyes.

Alain's baguettes were the real deal and I think even the Boss was impressed. We sat down and had baguettes and tea around Alain's kitchen table. He was quite the host was our Alain. Napkins and tea and butter and several types of jam and a little cheese were available for us.

The Boss started to interview Alain again, although he did stipulate that Alain was only helping us with our enquiries and was not, at this point, a suspect.

It made Alain feel a little better and he became just a little conspiratorial as if we were all on the same side.

The Boss recapped what Alain had said during his interview.

"Alain, you indicated you had a relationship, a sexual relationship with several men members of the group."

"Yes!"

"I believe you said you had sex with Eric, the victim, Art and Robin. What about Michael and Anthony?"

"Eric, Art and Robin. Robin only once or twice, I think. Athony no, but Michael, yes.

"Yet you didn't mention Michael at our first interview."

"If I committed or omitted Michael, it was a mistake on my part."

"Have you seen any of these people who were at the party since the murder took place?"

"Oh, yes. I have seen Art and his wife Becky. They have been here twice, since. Art has been here a few times alone. Michael and Lorraine just once, and Robin and Estelle possibly twice together and Robin has been here once on his own."

"And what was the general discussion about?"

"It is usually a rule that when the house has visitors, I should make myself vacant. You would say, disappear?"

"So you have no idea what was discussed with the visitors?"

"There are times when tea and baguettes are not enough, but I see the curtains being drawn sometimes."

"With everybody?"

"Not with everybody and not all of the time. But, there are some people who may come alone, and the curtains are sometimes drawn and sometimes they are not."

The Boss and I looked at each other. We had to ask the next question but before we could Alain continued, "Inspector, you want to know who the curtains are closed with. I would say Art has the curtains closed, Michael the same. I forgot that Estelle has been here alone. She had the curtains closed. Others I cannot recall. Oh also, when the funeral was being held, I was expected to stay here and cook for the people who came back afterwards. Perhaps there were fifty people. Maybe 60 people but not less than thirty. It is no matter that I also grieved for the loss of a dear friend! I was here as a, how you would say, chief cook and bottle washer. Not a good way."

The Boss continued, "Alain you said your boss was at Herbay. Where is that?"

"Pardon my poor pronunciation, I am told it is Herne Bay. It is in Auckland? She is staying with her sister?"

"Thank you very much for going over all of this. I can appreciate you are also grieving. Will you be staying on here in this capacity, er this job?"

"I do not know. The lady has made it very clear she would want me to stay but only as a butler person. Although, she has been to see me twice when she felt just a little lonely."

"Apologies, Alain, but I have to ask. Did these visits involve sex?"

"But of course. She is a very highly sexual woman. If she uses me, who am I to complain if it gives her just a little comfort. You look suspicious, Inspector. I have said it before. It is the French way of doing things."

The Boss thanked Alain for his baguettes, his tea and his questions. I think the Boss was just a little confused as to the very casual nature of sex that the French have. Definitely not a Kiwi thing. Come to think of it, it's definitely not an English thing either!

On the way back to the station the Boss and I were discussing the morning and our chat with Alain. The Boss decided he might have more success going with only the blokes who had sex with the victim. At the very least it would cut the suspect list in half! Yes we had already had this conversation but I readily agreed with the Boss.

On arriving back to the station I was greeted by the two DCs. One case of GBH and the victim was recovering in hospital with the assailant already locked away in the cells over the road. The other two were a retail burglary and a commercial burglary. Both cases looked like an inside job. To be fair the DCs looked at the situation quite carefully. No forced entry. No fingerprints. The robber knew what he was looking for. It looked like an open and shut case. But I had a feeling.

Between us the Boss and I updated the Sarge on how our session with Alain had gone. Like us, the Sarge was amazed at the casual attitude the French had with sex and was wondering what had gone on behind closed curtains at Hamurana. For myself, if the curtains are closed I don't really have any interest. With the Sarge there was always a possibility of just a little hanky panky going on and that added spice to his life.

We had a meeting with the two DCs and the Sarge to review our current case load. We had a rash of commercial and retail burglaries that seemed to be inside jobs. We had a murder case, and we had a stream of ram raids that remained unsolved.

Starting with the murder case we all agreed with the Boss that looking for the murderer was probably best sorted by focusing on the male members of the partygoers. The Boss gave his interpretation of what Alain had said this morning. It wasn't a lot of help either way, but it did give us an insight to how the minds of these people worked.

With the ram raids, the Boss had come up with a plan. Instead of booking the spare lads into a motel, could we possibly accommodate them with our own lads as billets. If we parked the squad cars at the big nick across the road and then didn't gather until perhaps six o'clock, it might give us the element of surprise? It was something the Boss wanted to try out so he would go over to the Squaddies briefing on Tuesday and see how they felt about billeting the spare lads.

The he remembered he was supposed to be taking Tuesday off. Sod it. He'd take Wednesday off. Once he had an idea in his head, he was like a bulldog with a bone.

I asked the assembled group to leave the Inside commercial and retail burglaries to me to handle. I had a vague suspicion, but I had yet to formulate a plan. Normally, it would come to me in the middle of the night, but it was usually worth it.

It was getting to the end of the day, so the Boss called It. The two DCs were taking Tuesday off so they were happy. The Boss reckoned he was taking Wednesday off so he was happy. As for me I'd worked for two weeks straight, or was it three weeks, with just the Sunday off, but no one seemed to care.

I made a half-hearted plan to go and see one of my confidential informants the next day. That usually brightened my day. Yes, tomorrow I'd try and do that!

It was about 3 am when I woke up and then I wondered what I had been dreaming about. The rash of burglaries, that was it. What if they weren't inside jobs? What if we had a mastermind that had keys to every building in town? My mind went along this track for the next few minutes until I drifted off to sleep again. Never mind. Once it was in my brain, I'd remember it!

Chapter 8

Tuesday

I'd gone back to sleep easily at 3.00am and when the Boss rang me at 4.00am I was convinced it was a part of my dream. It wasn't!

The Boss reckoned he had a call from the station and he could pass it on to me as it sounded like it was connected to my weedkiller lad. Only this time he had set fire to a classroom at Western Heights intermediate. I said thanks to the Boss and got out of bed on autopilot. Then the phone rang again. On a positive note I was marginally more awake. This time it was the lads from the Fire Brigade. The callout they had received from Western Heights sounded like I might be interested. They had a good crowd gathered of neighbours and they had a video going. I said I was on my way and he gave me instructions on where the classroom was ablaze.

On the drive up I was trying to remember whether I had ever had an arson case before. I couldn't recall so I was not really prepared for the scene of the blaze. I was probably two or three streets away when I noticed the flames towering above everything else. I parked on the road and made my way towards the fire. I found the guy in charge of the Brigade and introduced myself.

"There's a heavy smell of petrol around and we probably won't be able to stop it spreading to the next building, another classroom. If we soak the main fire and then focus on the next door we may be able to minimize the damage, but it looks like they'll be short of a couple of classrooms by morning. Glad we got your call. So who do you fancy as an arsonist?" he spread his arm out at the crowd gathered.

As I followed his arm I could see there was probably a 100 or more people watching the fire. Neighbours woken up by the noise of flames and the fire engines. I could only hope my arsonist was among the spectators. The Inspector suggested I bugger off as I could do nothing until the fire was out and that would be at least another two hours.

"Go home and get some kip. I'll be back at the scene by nine am. Shall we meet then?"

I agreed and went home where I slept fitfully for another hour or so before finally giving up the idea of sleep.

In at my usual time on Tuesday I was reminded by the Sarge that it was my job to go and get the coffees. It was another late summer's day. Hang on, the clocks have gone back. Does that mean it is autumn? Whatever, it was a gloriously sunny day with a possibility of a light frost that night. I almost forgot I had a broken sleep until I got over to the coffee shop and Annie mentioned I had looked better on other days!

Back in the office I hit the Sarge with my thought about the arson. It was the first the Sarge had heard about it. He let me say what I had to say and he and I discussed the situation for ten minutes before I realised I had another appointment.

I had to meet the guy from the Brigade at 9.00 am so I went up there and left the Sarge thinking over my thoughts on the Burglaries.

The Inspector from the fire brigade was already on site when I arrived. I left him alone to do his investigations while I chatted to the headmaster. The headmaster was very agitated. First off he was worried about why anyone would pick his school out. Then he went on about how he would struggle to find temporary accommodation for the classes. As the main target had been the art classroom he was less concerned than if it had been the science place where dangerous chemicals may have been stored. To be honest I was getting a bit teed off with the headmaster and I was grateful to excuse myself and meet up with the Inspector once he had completed his investigations.

"It's not that hard to work out. The guy spread petrol around the classroom and then lit a match. There is a lot of damage and also to the place next door. The main damage is to the art room and the secondary damage to the neighboring room. Both will need a rebuild. That's after a demo job first. I suppose you'd like to see the video we took?"

"Thanks Inspector. I'd prefer it if we could have a copy. Then we'll have to show it to the headmaster so he can identify locals and the like."

Oddly the fire service investigator was a little chattier with me. He reckoned the guy who did the arson was an amateur. When I asked him to explain he reckoned that that the arsonist had liberally spread petrol everywhere in the room. I can't quote the guy as he was spouting technical terms like 'limits of conflagration' at me but the gist of what he said was this. Petrol gave off a vapor and didn't really need to be spread over the room. When the arsonist had lit a match the entire room would have gone up in flames and if the arsonist was really lucky he might have got off with singed eyebrows. In a worst case scenario we might have found the charred remains of the arsonist in the fire ashes. I said I was surprised at that. He reckoned I would not be as surprised as the guy when he tossed a match at the petrol!

"I'll have a full report on your desk by tomorrow. Okay if we sort the video at the same time?"

"That's perfect. I'll wait until I hear from you."

I went back to the station. My plans on giving the weed killer guy to Tim and Dave had gone well awry as they were tied up with the ram raid duty. I really needed this extra case like a hole in the head! I already had a murder case and a possible lockpicker showing his skills! The Boss and the two DC's were busy doing the extra work for the ram raiders. It seemed to be a busy time for the CIB lads!

I sat down with the Sarge. I had remembered about my thoughts at 3.00am about the burglaries. Okay, he might have dismissed my thoughts about the mastermind having keys to every place in town. He may also have mentioned it as a plot line for 'Despicable Me'. We did eventually sit down and nut out who the possible suggestions for 'Despicable Me' might be.

An experienced locksmith?

A security firm technician?

A guy who repaired and replaced locks for a living?

An experienced locksmith was the first choice, mainly because we had not had an alarm at all of the break-ins. To check on the third guy we would have to ask if the burglary victims had recently had a lock replaced. I started to prepare a list of questions I could go and ask the burglary victims. The Sarge reminded me that the two DCs were not in today, so I was covering todays CIB cases. No, I was thrilled. Absolutely thrilled!

Then the Boss walked in the door. He had received a good welcome during the squaddies briefing. When he asked who could accommodate the spare lads, he had it pretty well filled up without too much bother. Now his next problem would be to sell the idea to the spare lads who would be coming over. Don't get me wrong but when a Police officer is on temporary transfer to a new station, they have to be accommodated in a place that fits in with their rank. And the higher up the pecking order you are the higher the quality of accommodation is expected. The Boss spent an hour on the phone, and it was all settled. Only one of the original lads couldn't make it this weekend because he had a family thing to attend. All of the rest were quite happy to bunk in with a billet. It was decided we would do the Friday and Saturday night again so that meant the Boss spent the next hour back on the phone again teeing it all up. We wouldn't meet util 6.30 pm and then we'd do it all by phone calls so we would have no possible leak of where our spare lads were going to be.

The Sarge reported in with the jobs wanting CIB input. Nothing! Thank goodness! That left me fairly free for the day. This morning I'd chase up my hunch on the burglaries and this afternoon I'd come up with something to do.

I had a brief recap of the burglary reports, both commercial and retail. Wow. There was a total of nine. Four retail and the other five were commercial. I hadn't known the total. Perhaps there was a trend developing.

Looking through the list in the yellow pages, the closest locksmith to me were the guys at Armstrong and Stott on Hinemoa Street. I wandered around to their shop and asked to speak to the manager. I gave the lady my business card and waited. It seemed like I was being whisked into the Boss's private office before I could be seen by anyone.

"Do we call you Mark or is it DS Hammell?"

When I really looked at the Boss, it was Anthony Stott, the guy from the party.

I said that Mark was fine.

"I suppose you've come to see me about the party?" said Anthony.

"No Actually I've come to..."

"Oh, So it's about the thing with Alain?"

"No Actually, it's about a different thing. Did you have something to say about the party? Or the thing with Alain"

"No, no, it's just unusual, to er... see someone from the Police. You know, so soon after the er... incidents."

"Let me get to the point. Perhaps you might like to add something afterwards, that might help us?"

"Oh, right!"

"I was here to ask you about a spate of burglaries we've had in Rotorua and ask for your input. Is it possible there is a locksmith in town capable of picking any lock in town?"

Now we were in Anthony's territory, and he seemed pleased to help me,

"Possible but not that likely. Every year we are told about a new lock on the market that is supposedly unpickable. All it takes is for a good locksmith to work out the pin mechanism and then it is usually not that hard to break."

"How many of these new types of lock would be fitted in a town like Rotorua?"

"Usually the cost is prohibitive, so I'd say very few. Perhaps three or maybe four. We're talking about a lock that would in excess of a couple of grand to install and then you have to get all of the new keys. Maybe up to three or four grand. Rotorua isn't that kind of place where everyone wants the latest security."

I enjoyed talking to Anthony. He certainly seemed to know his stuff.

"Okay. Those few locks aside, how many locks would a skilled lockpick be able to open?"

"At a pinch I'd say anything up to 90% or more for a good locksmith. An average guy, maybe 70%."

"So how could you tell if a lock had been picked?"

"Difficult. Usually there are scratches around the entry of the lock, that's what we would call the barrel or tumbler mechanism, but if the key has already made a scratch or two it's nigh on impossible to know."

"So it would be difficult to know if a lock had been picked?"

At this point I am really just thinking aloud. Anthony suggested that we go and look at a few locks. Being already on Hinemoa Street we got up and walked out to inspect a few recent cases of a possible 'inside job' within walking distance. The first two he decided it was impossible to say whether the lock had been picked or it had indeed been the use of a key. The last two he was sure it had been a lockpicker. But emphasized that it was just a hunch on his part. He did notice that all of the sites of entry were at a rear door. His comment was that it would give the lockpicker a few more minutes to work uninterrupted. My question was to the effect that there were good lockpicker lads in town and he was quite positive in saying he would estimate at least a half dozen and that was just the guys working for a registered locksmith. There were probably a few others that he knew that he wouldn't employ but they were also pretty good at lockpicking. Walking back to his shop, the conversation somehow switched back to the party. Alain had tried his hand with Anthony, but he didn't like the idea so nothing more had been mentioned by Alain. I thanked Anthony for his help and walked back to the office, deep in thought. That 'Alain tried his hand'. It's an English saying that means he might have hinted a suggestion or something to that effect.

By the time I returned to the office Anthony had already been on the phone. On returning his call, Anthony said he had been thinking. Most shopkeepers were creatures of habit. If they left the shop by the front door and then locked the front door, chances are they would have a good lock on the back door, but they may also have a simple bolt mechanism on the back door which would not show on the outside. I should check if any other shops had been lock picked but then they had a bolt system. That means the lockpicker would have just moved onto the next business along. It was something I hadn't thought of, so I resolved to investigate that idea.

I had my lunch with the Sarge and the Boss. Along the way we discussed the possibility of Alain's involvement with the murder and dismissed him again as a possible suspect. He was far too slight in build to have lifted Eric Johnson up over a beam while he staged the suicide.

While I was there, I did ask what made the Boss think it was a murder and not a suicide. The Boss grinned at me," It wasn't that hard. If you hadn't been all tied up with yourself about being at the damn party, you might have spotted it."

The Sarge was also interested in my question.

The Boss reluctantly relented, "Okay I did have a thought about the likely trajectory of a swinging body against the likely friction caused by the rope he had knotted around his neck. Then I thought if the silly sod had hung himself, he'd need a chair to stand on and then kick it away. The nearest chair was five feet away and neatly tucked under the table. Whoever did it didn't think it through, and they placed the chair back under the table. Detective handbook 101."

The Sarge gave a mock clap. Even though I hadn't spotted the chair, I like to think my mind was otherwise occupied.

The Boss had finished his lunch, so he was going to take another half day. He reckoned if the big Boss thought about it long enough he'd be okay with it.

As for me I had the commercial burglaries to sort out. Then I remembered I had promised myself a visit to my CI, Janet. So, I made the phone call to Janet, and we agreed a meeting time for later that afternoon.

I went to visit the scenes of the commercial burglaries and did my checking. This took longer than I anticipated due to the distance between the sites. Yes, it looked like all of them were likely to be a lockpicker, although I could not entirely rule out the possibility of an inside job.

So how was this guy operating? Forgive me, the gentler sex. I always think of an offender as a male until proven otherwise.

I'm going to assume it was a bloke. I don't know any of the local lock guys that have a lady working for them.

What else was it that Anthony had said. Oh, yes. Check out those properties that had a simple hasp and thing arrangement. There was probably a correct name for the thing that secures the hasp, but I can't for the life of me think what it is! Is it a bolt?

Maybe I'll hope for a commercial or retail burglary in the morning. Then I can do some checking. I'll also have to go and check the previous sites where we have had burglaries that we dismissed as inside jobs.

With that, it was time to go and see my CI, Janet and check if she had anything to er... report.

And that nicely brought up my five o'clock. All in all, a productive sort of day.

Wednesday

I was quite looking forward to seeing if there were any commercial or retail burglaries. I wanted to test my theory, well Anthony's theory actually.

Fortunately there were two. I handed off the other cases to the DCs and I went to my burglary victims. One was a retail, and one was commercial. That was also becoming something of a pattern. Usually there was a commercial alongside a retail burglary across town. I put that thought in the back of my mind to check out later.

I went to the retail store first. Now I had an idea of what to look for, I went to the lock to see if there were tiny scratches at the key entry. It could still be either way. Then I had the brainwave. It happens that I might have the key to the mystery. I went to the business next door and asked them if I could examine their rear entry. It had a bolt! Then I went to the business on the other side. It didn't have a bolt. Going back to the business on the far side I asked the owner if he could check if the door lock itself was open or closed. It was open! The owner looked a little sheepish and says he might have forgotten to lock it. When I explained to him that the burglar next door might have tried to break into his place first and the simple fact, he had a bolt across the door might have made the burglar try next door, he was gob smacked! It appears I might have found the clue I was looking for. If the lock was picked and the burglar still could not open it, he would have to assume it had a bolt across on the inside. As he was working under cover of darkness, he could simply try the place next door and so on until he found a lock he could pick that did not have a bolt across. After that it simply became a crime of opportunity where he could grab whatever the business held in stock and get away. I stood back and surveyed the retail entry's until I could work out a pattern. The burglar was going for shops that had no alarms or cameras at the back door and there were plenty to choose from! After that he would simply pick the lock and try if there was a bolt across. I have to say I admired this burglar for his casual attitude. His lack of urgency almost helped him to commit the crimes.

Going back to the scene of the latest retail burglary I could confidently say that the owner had been the victim of a break-in and to make his report to his insurance company. I did get the fingerprint lads out to take whatever they could and also take some photos. But I didn't hold out much hope. If the guy was this well prepared and casual in his attitude, he would not be likely to leave any prints for us to pick up. This guy was most definitely a pro!

The commercial burglary was the same, now that I knew what I should be looking for. Again I had the fingerprint lads out but with little hope of a result. Still I felt pleased with myself for partly solving the case to the point where I at least knew the burglars M.O.

Now I had something to work with I could go back to the office. I filled in my report while I waited for the two DCs to get back. When they were back, I filled them in on what I had found and asked them to go back to the 'Inside jobs' we had covered for the last two weeks and ask the neighbours if they could remember that their back door had been unlocked and if they had a bolt across inside the back door. I had shared this info with the Sarge before the DCs had got back. He was just a little impressed, impressed that I had done my digging and asked the professional, Anthony Stott, what to look for.

At that point the guy from the Fire Brigade walked into our office. He had a full copy of the video footage and also he had completed his work on the report. He was something of an economist with words and his report was pretty much done with not a lot of excessive wordplay. He waited while we both watched the video footage of the crime. He couldn't add a lot to the footage other than describing the way his team had put out the fire. As I said he was not the guy for making a big speech when a small one would do!

While he was there the Inspector also had a copy of the local paper and the police and Fire Brigade had made the front page. The local paper had a big article headlining the news about the fire at the school yesterday. Yes, they had photos of kids crying and a local kid who had always dreamed of being an artist and whose own work had been featured in the local calendar sold by the school. If you want to, about now it's the time you might call me cynical for not believing everything the local paper says, but I digress. The local fire brigade had been asked for a quote and they had obliged. The local police had been approached and they had received short notice. Knowing the big Boss was away and they had probably rang the DI at home for a comment, I'm not surprised they got short notice!

I rang the headmaster from the Western Heights intermediate and said I would be up there at 1.00 with the video. Then I sat and had lunch with the Sarge. He was still saying he loved his boat but also he reckoned he might be a dab hand at this golf thing. I left him with that thought as I went to see the head at Western Heights.

He was just a shade this side of useless! He was one of those guys who focused on the kids and not so much with meeting the parents. He was not the ideal guy to have looking at a video of the onlookers at the fire!

I left him to ask the teaching staff to take a look at the video and said I would be back the next day.

I also had a couple of businesses who had been burgled, where I had attended as the CIB, so I spent the rest of the afternoon backtracking those cases. Then I went back to the office and tried to work on a timeline of crimes. How often was this lad going out? Did he have a preferred night? How come he usually did a commercial and then a retail, or vice versa? Was he fencing the gear or selling privately through the pubs etc? For a change I was quite engrossed in my work and the answers were not long in appearing. I realised that the Boss standing over my shoulder was cramping my style a little. This is what I had gone into Police work for. I reckoned I should take my senior's exam as a sergeant and go for DI. I think I had enough experience. That reminded me I should send off for my Senior Sarge exam and see what it entailed. It's odd how these myriads of thoughts go through your brain when you are working on a good case. They don't detract from your thinking; they somehow add to it!

The Sarge gave me a nudge and reminded me it was after five. I went home and felt I had earned my few dollars today.

Thursday

In at my usual time I was ready to tell the Boss about my breakthrough. The DC brought the coffee over and I resumed working on what had been my task the previous afternoon.

The Boss walked in and was immediately called over to the big Boss's office. He had taken the day off yesterday so could expect the big Boss to have a moan about it. In fairness he had worked most of the weekend.

When the Boss arrived back at our office, he looked a little grim. He called the Sarge in for a closed-door discussion. When that was over, he called me in, alone. Again for a closed-door discussion

He was definitely looking a little like he had not had a day off and now he was ready to take on the world.

"Come in, Mark and sit down. First the good news. The Boss is taking a couple of weeks off to go and visit his wife's sister in Brisbane. When I said congratulations, he didn't seem that pleased. It seems he and his wife's sister don't get on that well. Something to do with the Māori's 'over there' are all modern in their thinking and he doesn't hold with that."

I couldn't help it. I added, "And that's the good news?"

"Yeah, and it gets worse. First off, I am nominally in charge when he's away so he spent five minutes telling me what I could and couldn't do. How much I could spend and who I could fire, which is no-one!"

I added, jokingly, "So my job is still safe then?"

The Boss added," That's what we need to talk about. What have you done that pisses him off so much?"

I couldn't exactly think of anything specific, or recent, and I said that.

The Boss continued, "Right. He had been speaking to his mate in Hamilton and said something about the undercovers here. His mate in Hamilton said he had no-one working in our area. He looked at me as if I should know. I said the first thing that came into my head. I told him I meant Tauranga. It was the Tauranga lads working undercover. He told me to sit down and then he got onto his opposite number in Tauranga. Obviously, he didn't know anything about it, and he said so. Then the Boss asked me who had been at the party that I was covering the murder case for. I had to say it was you and your girlfriend."

I added, "Oh, hell. That doesn't sound good!"

"Then he asked me who you really knew at the party. When I said it was your bird, he went apeshit. Reckons it was a no-no to get involved in wife swapping when you were on the force. I tried to tell him you went to the place as a dinner guest, but he wasn't having any of that. He did give you marks for excusing yourself from the case when you realised who everyone was but that was all he would give you. Last I spoke to him was that you should be out of this district if you were that well in with the locals. I'm telling you as a mate, Mark. The Boss has it in for you. Reckons he'll have a think about your future in his region over his holiday. He'll probably want a chat with you when he gets back. Sorry, mate but I reckon you're on the cards for a transfer."

I sat a little dejected for a moment.

"Don't worry about it Boss. If my future is dependent on him having a nice time on his holiday, I'm well scuppered!"

The Boss reckoned I needed a big win in breaking a case so he couldn't send me on. My reply was that a decent win could also give him the excuse to get me promoted and then move me on.

The Boss reckoned I should take the day off and plan my next move. The office was fairly quiet, and I wouldn't be missed. If the big Boss asked, the Boss would tell him, I was out on a case.

I thanked the Boss and said I would take the day off. but I might be back in later if that was okay.

As I tidied my desk up the phone rang. It was the police psych guy. He had read the coverage in the local paper and wanted to touch base with me. He reckoned the local coverage was better than I could have hoped for. Also in another part of the local rag there was coverage of the two more cases of weedkiller spray. There was an inference about the fire at the school being related to the weed killer guy but it was down to inference as they weren't getting anything from the big Boss. He had passed it on to my Boss and my Boss had ignored the call asking him to ring back. I spent a few minutes speaking to the psych guy asking him what I could expect. He reckoned it was unlikely the guy would try anything more for a week or so. Maybe even as long as three weeks, but he would like seeing his persona identified in the paper so he would most likely reoffend again.

As I passed the Sarge's desk, he said it might work out alright if the Boss had a decent holiday. I had nothing to say as I was fairly disappointed, so I went home. My arsonist was likely to reoffend. My lockpicker was enjoying his free rein and my murder case was still unsolved. No. I didn't have a lot to be happy about!

That afternoon I visited Tiff. I was in a down mood and Tiff would help me lift my mood and I wasn't really in the mood to talk to Janet. Tiff did manage to lift my mood.

Chapter 9

Friday

The Boss was away from tomorrow on his holiday. I didn't really expect a call but every time the internal phone rang, I was on high alert.

The Boss asked me if I wanted any more cases to take my mind off the job and I took the opportunity to fill him in on what I had discovered over the last couple of days. He reckoned that was good police work, but I wasn't really in the mood. He was also surprised we had a psychologist on the payroll and was pleased we had some sort of grasp on the guy's psyche. As a final thing the Boss reminded me, I was also back on duty for the Saturday shift at the CIB office. How wonderful!

I spent an hour or two going over my work the previous day. The perp I was looking at for the commercial and retail burglaries worked mostly on Tuesday and Wednesday evening. Usual time of the burglaries was later in the evening. Anything from 9.30 to midnight. I hadn't worked out if he was using a fence but that would probably take a few visits to our fences and secondhand shops to sort out. I was missing something. Why would the perp cover the days when we mostly had a light duty shift on? That could actually be the reason! Was he timing his activities to coincide with the times when we usually only had one squad car available on patrol. It seemed he was. Obviously, we would have more patrol cars out on our busy nights Thursday night through to Sunday night. Could I assume that the perp also had a knowledge of police operations procedure? Well, if he was a current locksmith, then he probably would have good knowledge of our operations, Wouldn't he?

It was certainly something to think about. I went back a few months to see if we had a rise in commercial and retail burglaries. There was a slight trend in this type of burglary going back over the last few months. I added these places to my list and then sorted them by type of business. Gift shops, appliance shops, tool shops, welding shops, perfume shops. It was a good list and fairly wide ranging. Now I felt I had a proper grasp on the person or perp. I had a sort of idea of what he wanted. I just had to get him in the act.

I decided to go and see Anthony Stott again and show him the list and addresses. I reckon he would have been bound by some sort of locksmiths oath or at least a register where he could not tell me what he knew, but it was worth a try.

While I was out in my car I swung around to the Western Heights Intermediate to get the tape back from the headmaster. There were only five people we could not readily identify as parents or neighbours of the fire. I took a note and thought I would get the Sarge to have a scan through it. He knew most of the villains in the area.

I drove around to Anthony's and parked. Fortunately, Anthony was not anywhere near as nervous when he saw me walk in the shop door. That was good for me because when people are nervous, they do tend to be a little more cautious when they are giving out information.

Anthony and I sat down in his office, and he took my list. "Everything here is easy to fence. Even the tools. Used or not there is usually a good market for a ready-made and hand built tool set. Have you tried the secondhand shops?"

I replied in the negative.

"Probably not a lot of value there. They're usually offering less than 20 cents in the dollar as value. Probably the pubs is where you'd have the most joy. Easy to turn over for a few dollars. A twenty or a hundred dollar bill can go a long way in a pub if you don't ask questions."

I asked Anthony, "You sound like you have a bit of knowledge about fencing stuff."

He replied, "Not really, but you have to admire the nerve of some villains who walk in here and expect us to give away information about security systems that a particular shop has. We say we'll meet them back in the business and discuss it there. Usually they decline but, on a few occasions, I have turned up to a business and the real owner has no idea why we are there. It does give them a bit of a warning they might expect a late-night visitor. And it helps with our image as well."

I thanked Anthony and walked back to the office. For whatever reason I was only mildly enthusiastic. I put it down to the Big Boss and the talk we may have when he returns.

The two DCs were ready to report in that they had also canvassed the neighboring businesses of recent victims of burglary. They had a couple of successful hits where the owner could remember being surprised that their lock had been so easily picked so we may have a general upgrade of businesses being a bit more aware of security. Hopefully Armstrong and Stott would get a bit of that business. They deserved it.

The spare lads were due today and the two Dc's had been roped into general CIB work as the Boss felt I might throw a sickie today. It takes more than the big Boss for me to have a sick day.

As the spare lads were not coming down until after the office closed, the Boss took a half day off, so he was ready to work until later in the evening. He was back just before 5.00 to touch base with Sarge and I.

That night was a kind of dream for the Boss. They roped in four ram raiders and the Boss was convinced they had the ringleaders or organizers. You do get a feel for when the perp is just one of the locals trying his hand, or when you actually have a brainy sort of guy who has the odds well worked out.

Saturday

When I went in for my Saturday shift, I grabbed my usual coffee from over the road and was surprised to see Tim Cross turn up for work. With the Boss's rearranging of the schedule Tim had just assumed he would be in and had turned up for work. I delegated and suggested that he fill the day in, and I would take a day off as I had earned it. For whatever reason, Tim agreed. Perhaps I might have pulled rank on him, but it was set that I had an unexpected day off. While I was wondering what to do with my day off, the phone rang, and it was from over the road at the new Station. It seems we had an unexplained body to deal with out the back of Hamurana. If this sounds familiar, it was. Given Tim's relative inexperience I got on the phone to the Boss. Ringing him before 10.00 in the morning on his day off is never a recommended routine and he told me to bugger off. When I mentioned it was the same address as the last murder, he sounded momentarily interested before saying, "No, you can deal with it. Sod the Boss. I'm in charge for the next fortnight, handle it!"

I got out to the address just after 10.30, and that was about twenty minutes before the Boss arrived unexpectedly. I was dealing with Lesley Johnson and interviewing her when the Boss arrived.

The Body was that of Alain. Evidently, she was in the occasional habit of popping over to Alain's for a coffee. When she had gone upstairs to Alain's flat she had found him in bed. When she tried to wake him, she discovered he was fully clothed and suffering from a bang on the head which had got blood all over the sheets. I don't know whether she was angry at the blood on the sheets or whether she had gone over for a little 'comfort'. Either way it had set her off and she had phoned the Cops and waited in her house for the squad car to arrive. The Squaddie had arrived at just before ten and rang back to the station immediately which was why the Boss, and I were both on the scene within five minutes of each other.

The Boss explained that my being there was a whole grey area which he didn't want to think about. Secondly, I had already interrupted his sleep in so why shouldn't he be there.

I carried on interviewing Lesley while the Boss went to look at the crime scene. He got back to me in about a quarter hour.

"Right, I've got the fingerprints lads on their way, and they will take the photos. Looks like a blunt force trauma to the back of the head. The victim may or may not have known the attacker. I might get Mike Miles into do this one a bit quicker. I don't want to wait until Monday afternoon. The Boss says I have the power to spend up to twenty grand so I might as well spend some of it."

"Ambulance?" I asked.

"Should be here in about half an hour. They have a car crash to attend to. Maybe an hour. What have you got from the widow Twankey?"

"Reckons she just went over for a coffee. It's a ritual they have. When he didn't show in the lounge she went into the bedroom and found him face down on the bed. Oh, she also reckons that he would usually be in his pyjamas. That was also a part of the ritual because they were friends. I'm not suggesting she came over for anything more than coffee and baguettes, but it wouldn't surprise me. Says she got dressed after ringing the police. Says she hasn't disturbed the scene other than her going into the bedroom, initially."

"Hmm?" said the Boss, as if he also did not totally believe she was going over for a quick baguette.

The Boss rang Mike Miles and asked him to do us a favour by coming in and getting the autopsy done on this as soon as he could. As soon as Mike heard it was the same address as the murder two or three weeks ago, Mike had no problems. As I say. Mike does love a good mystery!

The fingerprint lads arrived, and they set about doing their thing. On a stroke of luck, the Boss rang the photography lads and they were ok for a bit of overtime, so they were also on their way out to the scene of the crime. By 10.30am the ambulance had arrived and removed the body. I felt just a little sorry for Lesley Johnson. She was now truly alone in that big house of hers. That didn't make me any keener to comfort her though, so the Boss and I travelled back to the office in convoy.

The Boss was annoyed about the murder. He still had the 'spares' coming over for that night's session with the ram raiders.

He made an executive decision.

"Right, you get everyone in here tomorrow for an interview. That's all of those who were at the party. Oh and be sure and get that Lesley in. Make her the first if you can. I reckon she's not telling us everything she knows. As for me I'm going home to kip for an hour or two. If it's as good as last night, it will be a late one. Once you have them all lined up for tomorrow you may as well go home. Oh by the way we're both on tomorrow. I'd like you to be there for the interviews."

He may have noticed my slightly disappointed face. I had half a mind to go up to the golf club and see if I could get a game.

"Cheer up, lad. Tomorrow you're on overtime if the Boss is not calling the shots. I reckon we should get right onto this case. And there's no time like tomorrow."

"If you're going home for a kip, do you want me to liaise with Mike Miles about the autopsy?"

"Good thinking. Book the day as work. I'll sort it out next week." With that he was gone!

I spent the next hour or so ringing all who had been at the party to tee up a time to get them in tomorrow. As that was a Sunday it became something of a problem, but I did manage to get them all sorted for a Sunday interview. While waiting for Tim Cross to get back from his callout I noted that the fingerprint lads had done their work and got the prints on to our system. Without much hope I did run the prints through the system but drew a blank.

On the off-chance Mike had done his thing at the morgue I rang him. He said he was nearly finished, and I should come up to his office.

Mike and I have a different way of determining nearly finished. For me it's just about done. With Mike it means the body is still open and just wants sewing back together. Mike realised our differences and covered the body with a sheet. For me it was still a dead body that had been cut up but to Mike it was quite acceptable. We compromised and went into his office.

"Time of death between 9 and perhaps 11.00pm. Cause of death is blunt force trauma. Possibly with something blunt like a hammer or iron pipe. Did you see anything like that at the scene of the crime?"

I hadn't noticed anything, so I demurred.

Mike continued, "I have done a tox report, but we won't have it back until Tuesday. What else do you want? No sign of recent sex either way but he was probably used to backdoor stuff as his anal muscles were a little relaxed. The body is in average condition, average muscle tone. Possibly had a drink in the evening but again, I'll have to wait for the tox report. He wasn't that drunk so it may have been only the one."

I thanked Mike for coming in on a Saturday and he was dismissive," Not often do we get a case like this. Two murders a fortnight or so apart at the same address. Not something I'd want to miss."

With that I went home and prepared to work on the Sunday. I thought of ringing the Boss to suggest a later time, but I thought better of it as the Boss would only just have got his head down.

Sunday

In a bit later than my usual time. I stopped at the BP on Fenton St to get a coffee as the Library Café was not open on Sunday. I would have been in at 8.30. The Boss arrived at 9.30 complaining that last night was a bust. Only one ram raider was caught, and it was not related to any professional organisation. It was a couple of local lads and they decided to have a go. Unfortunately they got their car stuck in the doors of the dairy and they were still trying to untangle their motor when the Squaddies arrived. They would be dealt with through the courts, and they'd probably get a month inside as the courts were determined to help stamp this thing out and a month was the court's idea of being tough.

Right, our first interview was Lesley, the wife of the first murder victim from the party. She had actually discovered Alain's body in his flat and that's all we will say about her intentions.

It's probably easier for me to go through the questions the Boss asked and give their answers as a group sort of thing as the Boss asked them all pretty much the same questions. Oh and he also asked them both as a couple and, he asked them individually.

As an aside, he also asked if anyone minded that I was present, given that I had been at the original party, as it were. Only Michael thought about it for a second before he consented. The rest of them were quite happy. Perhaps I would corroborate who was bonking who?

"Where were you between 9.30 and midnight on Friday."

Lesley: Home.

Michael: Home office doing some paperwork.

Lorraine: Home watching TV alone.

Anthony: Home watching TV, went to bed at 10.30.

Brandy: Home watching Tv until 11.30.

Art: Having a drink with some mates. Probably too many to remember. By that I mean drinks!

Becky: Waiting for Art to get home. I did watch some telly, but I can't remember what I watched.

Robin: Watching TV with Estelle.

Estelle: Watching TV with Robin.

"This may be embarrassing for you, but please remember it is also embarrassing for me to ask this question. Did you have a sexual relationship with Alain Rocher?

Lesley: Yes at parties and perhaps once or twice more.

Michael: Definitely not!

Lorraine: Yes at the parties a few times.

Anthony: No, he did try his hand once but I told him I wasn't interested.

Brandy: At the parties once or twice.

Art: I'd have to think, yes there may have been an instance when I was too drunk to drive.

The Boss interjected, "Art, you're not answering the question."

Art: Yes. There was the odd occasion.

The Boss then asked Art. "So you are saying it was more than just the one time?"

Art: Yes. It might have been a few times but I can't remember when or how often.

Becky: Yes.

Robin: Yes, but it was just once. Not my thing really.

Estelle: Oh, yes, often, but just at the parties.

The Boss then asked, "May I also ask whether you had a relationship, a sexual relationship with Eric?"

Estelle: I don't know what to say to you. I had a sex thing with Eric and Lesley. At first it was a fun thing with Lesley, but then I got a little more into her and it was pleasant. Eric was ok in bed but I wouldn't say he was the best available at the parties.

Lesley: Yes, but not as often as you might think. It was complicated.

Michael: You'll find out anyway. Yes. Eric and I did try it once but that was it.

Lorraine: Yes but only at the parties.

Anthony: If everyone is being honest, Eric and I did try it. Once when I was too drunk to drive home.

Brandy: Yes.

Art: We were frequent friends and that is all I would add.

Becky: Yes at the parties.

Robin: Just the once, or twice Not my thing really but it did give Eric a lot of pleasure.

Estelle: Probably the same as everyone else. At parties but not outside that.

Did Alain or Eric have any enemies? We are treating the case as a possible double homicide so we would ask you to think carefully.

Lesley: Alain knew no one in Rotorua.

Michael: Not that I know of, but we didn't move in the same circles.

Lorraine: Not that I am aware of.

Anthony: Don't know. We were in different businesses so it's hard to tell.

Brandy: He was successful so it wouldn't surprise me if Eric had enemies.

Art: No he was such a sweetie.

Becky: They were both very good to me so I can't imagine any enemies.

Robin: Eric would have made a few enemies he was fairly ruthless. Alain, I didn't really know him that well.

Estelle: Not really. It's almost sad to talk of the dead when they are gone.

When they had all left, I'd have thought we were ready to go home but the Boss had his teeth into the case.

"Right. I reckon we can assume that all of the girls had bonked whoever was available on a given night. I still think we should be looking at the lads who were... I don't know, bonking seems like the wrong word for what they were doing. Any comments, Mark?"

"Stick with bonking. It covers it."

"Okay, so let's work out which of the blokes was bonking either of the victims."

By a process of elimination we came up with the following list.

	Eric	Alain	Michael	Anthony	Art	Robin
Eric		yes	yes	no	yes	Yes
Alain	Yes		Yes	no	yes	yes
Michael	yes					
Anthony	yes					
Art	yes					
Robin	yes					
Lesley	Eric	Prob	Prob	Prob	Prob	Prob

I don't know how accurate it would be, but it was only to give us an indication, as it were. Now I think about it, it was probably not that accurate as some blokes were iffy about admitting to a homosexual relationship.

It seems that Anthony was not into male-on-male sex but everyone else was willing to give it a go. Yes, I know some people reckoned they were 'too drunk to drive home' but what were they doing in Eric or Alain's bed in the first place. Come to think of it, where were their wives? Were they having a go with Lesley? That would answer a few questions.

Finally the Boss called it a day and we went home. The Boss didn't exactly say I could take the Monday off so I assumed I would be back in on Monday.

Monday

In bright and early, well maybe not so bright. The weather is turning just a touch towards winter. It's not quite so warm today and there is a hint of greyness in the clouds. I think I am summer person.

Sarge reminded me it was my turn to go and grab the coffees so I wandered over and spoke with Annie. She mentioned the murder which was unusual. She then produced the paper which had it in as front-page news! The local rag had also mentioned there had been another murder at the same address a few weeks ago. When I got back to the office, I mentioned it to the Sarge and between us we looked it up online. It seems that The widow Johnson had rang the paper and they had given it front page after they interviewed her on Sunday afternoon. None of her friends were mentioned and if you didn't know the details of the case it was almost like someone had it in for her and her late hubby. As for the poor French guy who lived there, well don't get me started! I didn't anticipate the Boss would take it well and he burst into the office ten minutes later demanding to know who the hell had leaked the story from our office. I was the obvious choice for inquisition, but he soon calmed down when he read the story online and the whole thing was reported as the widow trying to work out why she had been so unfortunate.

"So the Widow Twankey wants a bit of sympathy, does she. That's interesting."

If anyone is interested, the 'Widow Twankey' reference is a play written by Gilbert and Sullivan a hundred years ago. If I try and guess the play's actual title, I'll get a hundred letters correcting me, so I won't bother!

The Boss called a meeting for all of the staff over in our office and went through the details of Saturday's murder case. From now on the Boss and I would be working the murder and the two DCs would be handling anything else that came up. The Boss then went to his office and called me in. For a while we poured over the details of the case, and we realised we didn't have that much to go on. Someone had topped Alain while his back was turned. It had happened in his bedroom so was there something else about to happen? Could it be someone who was about to have sex with Alain and there was a change of mind, for whatever reason? Is it possible the assailant was armed with a weapon and Alain was trying to get into the bedroom to protect himself? Why would the widow Johnson call the papers and tell her side of the story? These were all questions we asked ourselves. In the end we decided to go and visit the scene of the crime again. We rang the widow Johnson and told her we were on our way. The Boss added that she should be available for further questions at some time during the crime investigation. The Boss was still convinced the widow knew a bit more than she was letting on!

On the drive out to Hamurana we went through a few scenarios. Lovers tiff gone wrong. Lesley was unhappy about Alain sleeping with other blokes. Maybe it was because he was sleeping with the other women? We wouldn't really know until we had the chance to sit down with her.

The Boss then had another thought. If Janet and I had been invited along, was it because someone else had not been up to scratch. Were there other couples who had been along, and they had a motive? I suggested it opened up a whole can of new worms, but the Boss was still quietly determined.

At the scene of the crime the Boss was meticulous. We went through a dozen different scenarios where Alain would have had his back turned to the assailant. Obviously, that meant I was playing the part of the victim and the Boss was the assailant. Nothing really hit that hard for us, so we had our interview with the widow Johnson and a cuppa over in the main house.

The Boss asked if anyone else had been along to the parties. It seemed that Geoff and Melanie had moved up to Auckland which left the vacancy around the dinner table. Only one couple had been invited before Janet and I. and that was a couple called Bill and Wilhelmina. The blokes had all been keen to have a crack at Wilhelminha, but it seems the girls had not been that interested in her hubby, Bill. By general consensus they had not been invited again. A couple of the girls had taken Bill upstairs and described him as 'ho-hum'. So they were simply not invited again. I did get an inference that a couple of the ladies wanted to get me upstairs and before I could answer, the Boss shut me down with 'he's very shy'.

On the way back to the office the Boss was fairly quiet, and I respected that.

When we got back to the office the Boss was immediately called over, by Jane, the big Boss's PA, to go through the mail that the Boss had received. Upon his return a couple of hours later he was amazed how much minutia the Boss had to deal with. According to Jane the Boss wanted to know everything that happened in his region and dealing with all of the mail was just the first part of him being thorough.

It was now getting on for 2.30 and the Boss and I had another meeting.

"I'd like to get this case solved before my Boss gets back. It might stand you in good stead, as well, if we get everything tidied up."

Personally I didn't hold out much hope, but I agreed with him.

Then the Boss asked if we could rule out any of the partygoers. After a lot of discussion, we agreed that for the most part each hubby and wife alibied each other. So that was not the best start. We both reckon Lesley had bonked most of the blokes there and probably most of the women as well.

Anthony, well no one had suggested he was into the Male-on-Male thing with sex.

So we had Michael, Art, and Robin, and could we also assume that Alain hadn't killed Eric? Given that Alain was so upset by the demise of Eric, I tended to rule him out but the Boss was still holding out for him as a suspect.

We were still convinced, though, that Alain would not have had the strength to stage the suicide after strangling Eric, so we put him off to one side. To be honest neither of us were putting him too far to the side as it's amazing what an assailant can achieve when they get their adrenalin levels up.

Okay, so we had Michael, Art, and Robin. Could we rule any of them out.

Michael: Home doing paperwork in his office.

Art: Out on the booze, reckons he had no idea who he was with. Too much booze.

Robin: Home watching tv with wife, Estelle. Although they both alibied each other that can often be a giveaway and, well, it makes me a little suspicious.

The Boss summed up, "So they all had an alibi. They all reckon Eric had no real enemies and Alain was too local to Hamurana to have enemies. They all had sex with Alain and probably Eric. Have we progressed this case at all?"

"Not in the slightest!" I added.

"Leave me to do some thinking. Any progress with your commercial burglaries yet?" asked the Boss

"Not really. I reckon we're dealing with a good lock pick artist."

"So have you rung around the security firms and got ideas for who could do this? Could be an employee or an independent. Could be someone who has a freelance idea, you know, one of our customers? Maybe even a retired lockpicker? Maybe looking to eke out his pension?"

I thought about the Boss's suggestions, but as it was already close to 5.00pm we called it and went home.

Chapter 10

Tuesday

On Tuesday it finally hit me. I'd worked the last three weeks with only a couple of days off. I thought about a sickie but decided against it. Maybe I'd ask the Boss for a day off or a long weekend off, but not today. We were too busy!

I got in at my usual time and even the Sarge reckoned I should ask for a day off which was a bit rich as he got two days off every weekend, but it did firm up my resolve to mention it to the Boss when he came in.

I went over for the coffee and had a sit down with the Sarge where we talked about his fishing and my golf, or lack thereof!

When the Boss came in around 10.00, I was prepared to ask for a day off when the Boss remembered it was about time, I had a day off. If I took Wednesday off and he took Thursday off. It should work out fine. Getting down to the day, it transpired that the Boss had been over and sorted out all the post for the big Boss during his absence before coming over to our office. Yes, it made me feel just a little guilty about the day off.

I rang the Springfield pro about a tee time for the following day, he told me to come in at 9.00am and he would sort me out. So I had my day off well planned when the Boss came into my cubicle and asked me what I had on for the day. With my reply of, "Nothing. Just doing a recap of the recent cases" he asked me to accompany him out to Hamurana. He reckoned that something didn't add up with the details.

I happily got into his motor, and we went out to the scene of the crime, or in this case, both of the crimes!

His perplexment centered around the location of the house and the garage where Alain had his flat and the fact that it was at least 100 meters to the road where there was a gate that was usually shut.

When we got to the driveway, we noticed that the gate was open. The Boss was being picky, and we got out to look for tyre marks or something where a vehicle may have parked while they opened the gate.

There was nothing of note as we were in the middle of a fairly dry spell and fresh tyre marks would not have been left.

When we got to the house, Mrs. Johnson was already outside and wondering who the people at her gate were. We met her and the Boss asked her if she remembered any noises coming from outside her house the previous Friday night. She remembered nothing which was not a lot of use. She did think that if anyone had driven up the drive she would not have heard. She had watched the TV until around 10.30 and then gone to bed. That being said she did admit that she was getting into the habit of having a drink or perhaps a couple of drinks before she went to bed. Reckoned it helped her sleep now she was on her own. When pushed by the Boss she did admit that she often had a drink to help her relax even before Alain was murdered.

The Boss was still not ready to enter Alain's flat, so we had a walk around the yard and into the fields adjacent to the house and then followed it along the side of the driveway. We found it eventually. The murder weapon! It was a solid piece of pipe. Metal pipe. About two foot long and perhaps a couple of inches wide. For the metric minded among us that would probably be about 60 centimeters long and five centimeters wide. It had been tossed into a field and it had what looked like traces of blood on it. The Boss had me bag it up and place it in the back of his car to take back for forensics. It was easy to see that the piece of pipe had been tossed into the field as the assailant had been walking back to his car parked at the entrance to the driveway. The pipe looked like it was something that had been cut from the lengths of pipe around the side of the garage where the first victim had been building his cattle crush. A good murder weapon and quite heavy.

With the possible weapon in hand we now had something on which to develop our theories. Probably not a crime of pre-planning. An opportunity crime where the assailant had grabbed the pipe as he walked up the stairs, perhaps. Now that we looked at the scene with fresh eyes we could see where there was quite a bit of pipe around the side of the garage. Interesting how quickly the grass had grown around the side of the garage once Eric had been stopped from completing his work on the cattle crush. It was only a few weeks ago since Eric had been killed and the grass was already six inches high.

Going upstairs to the flat we could use our imagination and work out what had happened. Evidently Alain and his assailant had an argument and the assailant had walloped Alain over the head from behind. Looking at things from a positive note it must have been someone that Alain felt comfortable turning his back on. Possibly one of the three guys we had earmarked.

The Boss felt much more comfortable as we went back to the office. Now he had the method tied up he was always just a bit more comfortable.

When we got back to the office, I had my lunch, and the Boss went over to spend time doing more bits and pieces that Jane had rung about. I think he must have had lunch at the new cafeteria as he was quite chipper when he got back around 3.00pm.

I spent the afternoon compiling a list of where the commercial and retail burglaries had happened. I couldn't see a pattern emerging as they were all across town. The two DC's were in the office, so I peppered them with questions. Eventually they came and joined me, so my questions were better answered. By the time 5.00pm came around I discovered I had most of the files sitting on my desk. One of the DCs had made an itemized list of everything we believed this guy had got away with. It was quite impressive. Everything from watches to small appliances to tools to used toolboxes complete with tools. This guy was taking anything he reckoned he could get a few dollars for.

On my way home I realised I had spent another day with barely even a thought about the arson case or the weedkiller spray guy. Tomorrow I should do something about that.

Wednesday

Wednesday was my well-deserved day off. I had a game booked in at 9.00am at the golf club and I was hoping against hope that I would not get a call from the office telling me I was needed.

Luck was with me as I turned into the Springfield Golf club just before 9.00. It's quite an impressive sight as you drive in with the 16th hole unfolding on the left and the club itself right in front of you..

I got my clubs out of the car, and I spotted Art, the guy from the party. He walked up to me and whispered, "We met at a dinner party a week or so back. It was just dinner, OK?"

I greeted Art as warmly as I could, and I was introduced to the other guys I would be playing with. I'd love to say that Art felt very down, and he confessed everything to me as we walked down the fairway, but that only happens in Agatha Christie stuff. I had a very pleasant morning on a very nice sunny day playing golf with four like-minded individuals. I shot a 110 which after my handicap wasn't too bad. Art may have won, which was fine. In golf you should mainly focus on playing yourself and trying to beat your own handicap.

None the less I had a good morning.

I went back home for lunch and thought I would contact one of my CI's to see if they had anything to report in. You know what that means, I went to spend some time with Janet.

Janet, it's odd but I quite like spending time with Janet. It's like visiting an old friend. With benefits!

Janet and I talked about the case, the murder case, and I filled her in about Alain being also killed. She was fascinated! She was quite happy to spend her time talking about the case but that wasn't really what I was there for. Men have a completely different view on sex. Women want to talk about a topic. If there is the slightest chance of nudity on offer, men want to get down to it!

We talked for an hour or so about the details of both the first and the second case. This was among other things we dealt with, so it probably took the better part of three hours. As I was leaving Janet asked me to keep her up to speed on the case. I promised to do that, and we parted ways.

Thursday

It was only when I got in that the Sarge reminded me the Boss was taking a day off. I had forgotten!

Going over to get the coffee I sat down with the Sarge and had our drinks. Yesterday had been fairly quiet. The DCs had another two burglaries. Exactly the same set up. The lock was picked, and entry was made. When they went to investigate, they realised the connection with my earlier case, so they went to the neighbours. Same thing. One commercial had had the lock picked but it had a hasp thing, so they had simply moved next door and got into that place.

With the Boss not coming in and the two DCs taking the cases for CIB input I had a fairly quiet day. The Crown prosecutor wanted to speak to the Boss, but he ended up with me. They had a two-day trial set down for Monday where they would need one of the two or both DCs. It was related to the ram raid villains and that was not for me to deal with. The Boss and I would take on the cases from over the road. I set down to go over the cases in hand. I had a couple of murders on my desk and a spate of lock picking cases. Given that I had the lock picking cases already out I went with them first.

Still I could not detect any pattern. Still the guy seemed to be picking random streets. I turned to the total list of items the guy had got away with. It was quite impressive. When you added the previous days haul it was getting more and more so.

I turned my attention to where the guy would be fencing this stuff. He had to get rid of it somewhere. Maybe it was time I wandered around the secondhand shops and see if there was any newer items that warranted closer inspection.

We knew most of the lads that were into receiving stolen goods. Most often they had been nicked beforehand but there was the occasional guy we had not caught in the act. There was a new secondhand shop in town. Maybe I would spend the day wandering around town to see if I could spot anything.

Well what seemed like a great idea turned out to be a bust. I developed the habit of wandering around the place before I introduced myself. It's amazing how many of them take a furtive look around until they realise, I am watching them. Then they tend to get a little secretive with me. By the time 4.30 rolled around I had been in every secondhand dealer in town and come up with nothing. By this time, I was thinking that the guy must be fencing the stuff out of town. Was it worth my while to go over to Tauranga or Hamilton to see if any of the flea markets there were dealing in Rotorua's stolen goods? It was something I would speak with the Boss about when he returned. I went back to the office and went home a little after 5.00.

Friday

The Boss was in bright and early on Friday. He beat me in and then asked me if I had enjoyed my day off playing my round of golf. I told him about my meeting with Art from the party and the Boss was dismissive. If that's the lad that did them in, he'll give himself away soon enough. Then he surprised me with, "I went up to your Club yesterday. Had a lesson from what's his name? Wayne? He reckons I'm a natural with a tendency to hook the ball. Reckons once I learn to control that I should be down to an 18 handicap, whatever that Is? Maybe you and me should get out and have a game sometime."

With that the phone rang. It was Jane and the Sarge put it through to my desk as he spotted the Boss talking to me.

"Yes! No I had a day off yesterday. It's allowed when you put in a six- or seven-day week!"

Silence from the Boss's end.

"No Jane. I'll be there in about five minutes. Yes, thank you."

I knew better than to ask the Boss how his day was going. He simply said, "In the immortal words of Arnold Schwarzenegger, I'll be back!"

It must have been a good hour later when the Boss returned, "I've just shown Jane what crap the Boss deals with every day. I reckon she might have a go at him when he gets back."

Going into his office, the Boss shut his door and got on the phone.

The Sarge happened to be walking past my desk when he said, "It will never happen. The big Boss revels in the minutia. I reckon that's how he gets his jollies knowing everything that happens around his patch."

I hadn't been to see Ronnie or the Chinese for a week or so. Maybe it was time to renew their acquaintance. It's always good to know the gossip in your town. I was a little withdrawn from the Elders and the maraes. Putting one of their big names away had not gone down too well. Maybe I'd give them a wide berth for a while. There is rarely a few months go by when the big Boss is not urging us to support their marae, so I'd show my face next time the big Boss was around.

I went to see Ronnie first. I quite liked Ronnie. He was very no nonsense when he wanted to be, but he and I could usually get on ok.

I rang him first and told him I was coming. As always, he said he'd have the jug on when I arrived.

Ronnie and I sat down and chatted. There are many things I won't speak about to the likes of Ronnie, but Ronnie was different. He told me whether his drug sales were up or down that month. Where the scenes of aggro may occur. If I had something to mention such as a mob member being a bit aggressive with anyone, I'd mention it to Ronnie, and he would attend to it. There was a line we didn't cross but

I still liked Ronnie. In our chats he would mention something that it would be rude to write down in a notebook. I'd remember it for later, but it was a mutually beneficial relationship. While I was at Ronnie's I remembered I had done nothing on the arson case. I drove around there and popped in to see the headmaster. He assumed that his was the only case I had to deal with so he was happy to see me. He was having difficulty getting the assessor to come and recommend that the arsoned buildings be demolished and rebuilt. I sympathized with him and left him alone and went back to have lunch with the Sarge.

That afternoon I went to see Shi Low on Eruera St.

We had a nice cup of tea together while outside his office the locals were playing mahjong. I didn't get anything from Shi Low, but it was still a positive in terms of keeping in contact with local groups. I'll let you into a little secret. I actually enjoyed going to see Shi Low. He was always very polite and cordial but he kept me on my toes when I was speaking to him. I liked that.

When I got back to the office the Boss was still poring over all of the notes we had from the second murder case. He also had in mind of all of the info from the first murder case. I went into his office, but he was in a mind to go through all of his notes, so I left him alone.

I went back to my own cubicle and worked on the burglaries I had on file. Also it reminded me that I would need a new electric blanket for my bed. Yeah, as you get a bit older you do tend to feel the cold a bit more and the nights were getting a bit cooler.

I went on to Trade me. It's a Kiwi site where you can pick up a few bargains if you are careful. Having recently gone through all of these burglaries I had a good list of brand names to go for. I put in my search for a Phillips brand of electric blanket, and I straight away had a list of over a 100 lots of blankets for sale. I immediately thought this would be a great place to fence off stolen gear. Well, in my mind I quickly put one and one together and then started doing some digging. Starting with electric blankets, there was one for half price as an unwanted wedding present. Trade Me is a great site because you can quickly look up who the trader is and what else they may also have for sale. I had the trader flogging off an electric blanket. I also had him flogging off a retired mechanic's tool kit. I also, once I spent the time, had him selling a few more items that were also on our list of stolen goods. He'd be hard pressed to be selling an unwanted wedding present and at the same time he was also a retiring mechanic.

I could bookmark the traders name and then I went off looking for another item. A near new welding set. Not on the same traders site but on another site where the trader also had a few items for sale. Maybe over 50 items. By spending a bit of time I managed to get past 5.00 and went home. It may be a policeman thing but once I was home, I spent a bit more time on Trade Me. I was so wrapped up in my work it was after 9.00 when I realised the time. I was tempted to go into the office and pick up the list of stolen goods, but I fought off the temptation and watched a bit of You Tube on the topic of putting. It didn't really tell me anything I needed to know. It was a bit more on the Zen of putting! Don't let me get my head filled with the Zen of putting. All I wanted was to know how to get the ball in the hole!

Tomorrow was a Saturday, and no one had told me I was supposed to go into the office so I reckoned I would stay clear of the office and maybe go for a game of golf if the weather looked reasonable.

<u>Saturday</u>.

I went into the office around 10.00. Oddly the Boss was there along with Dave Powell. It seems that the Boss and Dave had made a mess of their timing and it was Dave's turn to deal with the Saturday. The Boss and I made a very quick decision to go for a game of golf so while I rang the pro to arrange a tee time, the Boss readied himself to meet Alain's sister. If we could get to Springfield by 11.45, we would have a tee time with a couple of other locals who were of a similar strength to the two of us.

At 10.30 Alain's sister arrived. We sat her down in the interview room and we listened to her speak, and then speak some more. It may be a Kiwi thing, but we are inclined to let the other person have a chance to get a word in edgewise. In France it seemed to be quite different. Eventually when she had run out of steam, we took everything she offered and prepared to go for our game of golf. She had gathered all sorts of papers and bank statements relating to Alain and dumped them on us. She had also organised to ship anything she considered of value over to France and wondered what we would do with the rest. The Boss told her very firmly that it was not our job to deal with Alain's estate and we would be doing nothing with it. The French are quite assertive in their own way and while she initially thought the Boss was quite rude, she did warm to him eventually and appreciated his way of talking. Evidently with the French Police it becomes a question of who assumes the most authority that has their way.

We bundle Alain's sister out of the office and were on our way to the golf course at a shade past 11.30. We both had to go and grab our clubs, so we were only just in time to make it to the first tee at 11.45.

Can I just say that I beat the Boss! By the time we were walking the long 15th hole I was already ahead, and the Boss had to resort to some risky shots to try and salvage the game. He failed and I won by something like ten shots as his play became more desperate. We didn't count the final hole as the Boss had something of major meltdown in his play. I think we even beat the players against us, but I was more satisfied with hiding my smirk of self-congratulations as I celebrated the win.

We had a quick beer at around 4.30 and then we went home. If the Boss had won, we might have gone back to the office but as I won, we went home. I enjoyed my evening and my Sunday off, and I went into the office on the Monday in a great mood.

Monday

It wasn't my turn to go and get the coffee so I sat with the Sarge, and I regaled him with my win. In hindsight it must be like me listening to the Sarge's fishing stories. We do it because we are polite! Weather wise it seemed like we were definitely getting into autumn with the temperatures having a cold edge on them in the morning and at night we were definitely getting closer to our first frost of the year!

The Sarge told me I had a visitor on the Friday. It was the Fire service boss giving me the report and the video. The Sarge reckoned he had twisted the truth just a little and I had been called out on an urgent case so I had been covered. If I recall I was meeting Janet. Well it made up for the work I did on Saturday!

The Boss wandered in at 8.00 and handed out the weekend's jobs to the two DCs and then he went into his office and set about the pile of paperwork left by Alain's sister. At 8.30 Jane rang from over the road for the Boss to come and attend to the big Boss's paperwork. With an excuse for an out, the Boss grabbed the pile of papers on his desk and dropped them onto my desk. "Here, grab a look at this lot," he said as he walked out of our office.

My initial thought was what a waste of my time and that the Boss had an out with big Boss going for his holidays. My second thought was that I had nothing else to do while the Boss was over the road so it would give me something to do. Going through what seemed like a mountain of paperwork was interesting. There were bank statements and visa statements and invoices for Alain's car repairs and visa receipts for Alain's purchases. Within a half hour I had a general picture of Alain's spending. He had very few costs as he mostly ate from the Johnson's kitchen. He spent a few dollars on clothes, and he had his car to sort out with WOF and petrol etc. Other than that he banked most of his salary that he received from the Johnsons. When I glanced at his bank account, he had over $31,000 in his credit. That's not bad for a factotum or butler or whatever he was called. I briefly wondered whether he would be staying on at the Johnsons until I remembered he was the victim of the second murder. Call it being lulled into a state of semi doziness when confronted by a stack of paperwork.

With a stack pf papers in front of me that must have been a couple of inches deep I decided I would get organised and sort everything into piles. It only took me around twenty minutes and by that time it was time for morning tea. I went and sat with the Sarge, and I regaled him with my tale of beating the Boss at golf on Saturday. He was quite chirpy as I told him about the Boss's game going to the pack when he tried to pull everything out of the bag to ensure an honorable draw or at least to minimize the defeat. After morning tea I went back to the piles of paperwork and got down to it.

Other than sorting his car out, which I later discovered belonged to the Johnsons, Alain had no real bills to deal with. His Visa card and his car were the main expenditures. Going through his bank statements I discovered that Alain was on $600 a week. I assumed he was not paying for the flat above the garage as I had seen nothing that indicated he was paying rent. It was a pure coincidence in that I looked at Alain's various bills before looking at his bank statements. When I eventually went over his bank statements, inside my head there were alarm bells ringing as in, "what the hell is going on here?'

It seemed that Alain was getting his $600 per week from the Johnsons. Plus he was also getting $250 a week, to be exact he was getting $250.97 from someone called PJH. When I looked forward in the statements, he was also getting another grand a month from a firm called AL Holdings Ltd. If nothing else, it added to Alain's overall mystery.

I couldn't work out who this PJH firm were or the other place AL Holdings Ltd.

I resolved to wait for the Boss with my findings. As luck would have it the Boss walked back into the office within a few moments of leaving it. The Boss immediately summoned me to his office, and I thought this can't be good.

The Boss got down to brass tacks immediately.

"My Boss is back, and he reckons he didn't have a great holiday. It appears he still has it in for you. He told me to arrange to get you transferred and I told him that was his job, and he would have to be the one to tell you to your face. Sorry, Mark, are you sure you don't know why he has it in for you?"

"Nothing I can think of Boss."

I knew why he wanted me gone. I was one of the few that could finger him for being a naughty lad as a beat cop. But surely, he wouldn't still be hanging on to that for all those years?

"Well he reckons he will get round to it one of these days. In the meantime he has to spend his precious time sorting out all of the messes I made while he was away!"

I was really disappointed with this outcome, but we hadn't solved the murder case and I was kind of pinning my hopes on that being solved.

"Okay, Boss, and thanks for sticking up for me. Moving right along, do you want to see what I have come up with?"

Going back to my desk I went through the piles of paperwork with him, leaving the bank statements until the last.

"So far it's a typical single blokes affairs with not a lot to comment on, until we get to the Bank Statements!"

I started to get excited and so did the Boss, "So you reckon he was getting 600 a week from the Johnsons. Plus, he was getting 250 odd every week from this other crowd and then he was getting another grand a month from who is this, AL Holdings Ltd? No wonder he has a decent back account. What does he have, good grief, he has over 30,000 in his account. That can't be legit, can it? He's on the best part of 100,000 grand a year and it's all tax free."

"So why is he getting it and who is he getting it from?"

"That, my friend, is what we have to find out. What are the names of those three blokes we had last week. What are the names of their companies?"

By going on the internet we found out the names of the three companies of our suspects from last week and we drew a blank.

"Right, go on the Company register and find out who are the shareholders of our companies. Let's see if we can find a link back to these lads. It's worth a try.

Going on the Companies register is a lot harder than we realised. It involves requesting a search and then waiting for a day to get the results. I did the paperwork and then sat back and waited for the results.

The Sarge was interested in our findings, so I sat down with him over lunch, and we discussed the case. During our chat the Sarge reckoned that Huia was getting a bit tired of always having fish for tea. He reckoned he would probably get as much as he paid for his boat. Maybe he would try his hand at golf? He reckoned it couldn't be that hard if the Boss and I were getting better at it.

That reminded me I hadn't told the Sarge I was up for a transfer. I reckoned it might be better to leave it for a while. I was still just a bit emotional about it, and still just a bit teed off with the big Boss!

In the afternoon we had a call from Lesley Johnson. It seemed that Alain's sister was getting some people in to give her a good price for Alain's stuff. Were we okay with her disturbing a crime scene? I got the strong impression that Lesley and Alain's sister were not getting on too well. I conferred with the Boss, and he agreed we should take one last look at the crime scene. I then left it to Lesley to tell Alain's sister to hold off until we got out to Hamurana the following morning. By the sound of it Lesley was the one having some difficulty in letting Alain and his stuff go. Nothing to do with me. I said to Lesley we would be out mid-morning tomorrow.

I should have anticipated that I would get a call from Alain's sister, but I simply told her that the Police in NZ do things differently and if she wanted to be more decisive to my face I could still arrange for it to be another couple of weeks before we released it as a crime scene. Not my most tactful moment but Alain's sister was beginning to get up my nose with her constant demanding that the world stops for her!

At 5.00 I went home and had a quiet night. The Boss got a phone call from Alain's sister, and he also was abrupt with her to the point of being rude. As for the Boss, I reckoned that Alain's sister quite fancied him.

Chapter 11

T<u>uesday</u>

In at my usual time, Dave had the day off, so Tim went over for the coffee. The Sarge and I were sitting talking when Tim returned. Tim was not the talkative type, so he went back to his desk while the Sarge and I carried on our chat.

Among the topics covered were the fact that many companies had a holding account for their company for tax purposes, if not just to make it easier to avoid trouble with the taxman. Also the Sarge had thought a bit more about taking up golf. He reckoned he would usually have someone to play with on a Saturday if either the Boss or I were covering a Saturday. Typical Sarge, he had thought it all through, other than getting a decent price for his boat. It was getting closer to the end of the boating season now. Would he still get a good price? He wasn't too concerned and reckoned he might take a day off and go up to the golf club and have a lesson. Once the Sarge had an idea in his head, it usually happened so I would next hear about his new clubs and his possibly selling his boat.

Just then the Boss walked in and enquired if I had heard from the Companies Office. When I checked we had got the notice, so I opened up the files.

PJH were the firm of Robyn & Estelle. It was the previous name of the company when they purchased it twenty years ago and they had decided to leave the name in place for the goodwill it may engender.

AL Holdings major shareholders were Art and his partner. I noted that Art was the major partner in a 1/3 and 2/3 shareholding.

From the new Info gained, the Boss and I sat down and wondered why they were both employing Alain. As far as I could tell Alain had been Robin's employee for around eight months and working for Art for around 6 months.

The Boss was more decisive, "Let's go and see these lads. If we turn up unannounced, they won't be able to prepare any dodgy stories. Come on, let's do it!"

Within a few moments we were on the road to Robins Engineering factory. We got there just after 9.00 and fortunately Estelle was in the office by then. We asked for a meeting with Robin, and he arrived from the workshop quite grubby and stained and in overalls. The Boss asked to meet with Robin, but Estelle wanted to stick around. Once again, the Boss was quite firm with her. Effectively he told her to bugger off! It might have been politely said but we all knew what he was saying. She walked off with something in her manner that was just a bit argumentative.

When we were sat down with Robin in his office the Boss came straight out with it. "Robin. You have employed Alain for a few months, maybe a year. Can we see his employment records. Hours worked, that type of thing. Salary scale. You know that type of thing."

Robin definitely looked worried. He said he would have to ask Estelle as she handled the books for the company. The Boss said he wasn't worried. If we had to get Estelle in, Robin was free to ask her to leave at any point.

Estelle arrived in Robin's office without being asked. The Boss asked Estelle if she had been listening to the conversation via the intercom on Robin's desk. Estelle at first denied it but then said she knew we would want her in soon enough.

The Boss was unfazed," So, where are Alain's employment records?"

"Apologies they are at the accountants. Yearend stuff. You know how it is."

The Boss was quite cool with her, "And you knew all of this without even checking your computer. About them being at the accountants? What if I said that's a load of garbage, Estelle. What if I said you'd have a copy, at least, of everything about the company. What if I said you were not trying to hide something from a Police enquiry? Well, are you?"

Estelle looked a little perturbed. She knew she had met her match with the Boss, "I might have something related to Alain's pay, if that would help."

The Boss's attention was now fixed on Estelle, "How about you tell me what hours Alain worked."

Robin was trying to help out. He added, "We used him as a cleaner. He'd come in and sweep the workshop out and stuff like that."

The Boss turned his attention to Robin, "So he came in after hours. What, sometime after five? Maybe he worked a couple of hours every night for your firm."

Robin was relieved, "Yes, that's it. He came in for a couple of hours after five o'clock. When he was done, he left."

The Boss looked unimpressed, but I knew from his face he was about to drop the trap. "So, Alain was here cleaning the workshop and at the same time he was also working at the Johnsons preparing their meal. To me, that doesn't sound quite right. How about we talk about the real reason Alain was on your books?"

Robin looked like he was beaten. Estelle knew she was caught. She was the first to speak.

"Okay, so the little French bastard was blackmailing us. Reckoned it might hurt our business if people knew what we got up to on weekends, and with Robin and Alain getting it on, that wouldn't have helped any."

"So how long was he blackmailing you for?" asked the Boss.

"Eight or nine months. He reckoned he was applying for a job with us and when we said we had no jobs for his skills, that's when he turned the screws on us."

Estelle looked defeated and Robin was close to tears as he could see his workplace folding along with their comfortable lifestyle.

The Boss asked, "Robin, and I include Estelle in this, did you kill Eric or Alain?"

Both of them denied it so the Boss thanked them for their eventual honesty, and we got up and left. Oh, and before we left the Boss asked them to forward Alain's employment records to his email.

I couldn't help it but congratulate the Boss on his assumptions and their subsequent admission of being blackmailed.

The Boss was quite chipper and said, "Now we go and see Art. Let's see if he wants to play 'pretend Alain works for me'. Where is his place?"

Art worked out of an office on the edge of town, close enough to be trendy but cheap enough to cut costs.

Art was not thrilled to see either of us, but he did usher into his office where it was quiet. Or perhaps it was where nobody could overhear our chat.

We hit Art that he had an employee named Alain, possibly a part time worker. After a second or two of thinking Art figured that we were talking about Alain, the murder victim. The whole thing was a charade to the Boss and I, but we did ask what job Alain did for Art. "He's a postman. When the surveyor goes out to check a property, the Surveyor is on the theodolite and the postman holds the sighting tool when we have to check the gradients and the like. He didn't work that much for us, but he was a handy bloke to have around."

The Boss was only waiting to pounce, "Art, so you are saying that Alain worked infrequently for you?"

Art was pleased to think he had the Boss's questions covered, "Yeah. It would be something like that. Whenever we needed him he would come in."

The Boss waited for Art to settle down before he asked his next question, "But his pay was the same every week, that sounds like he was a regular worker, to me? Am I getting something wrong here?"

"If his pay was the same, then he must have worked odd hours but they probably all totaled up to the same amount. Every week you say. That is interesting and, obviously, a coincidence."

The Boss now had his serious face on and he looked Art in the eye, "Art, I put it to you that Alain was blackmailing you and you put his money through the firm's accounts for whatever reason?"

Art knew he was beaten. He sighed and said. "Yes, the sod was greasing for cash. Said he wanted a grand a month or he'd let it out that I was doing Eric and stuff. Don't talk to me about what goes on outside and everyone reckons we should be praising the gays for their bravery. Here in little old New Zealand we still reckon anyone who is bent is to be avoided. I don't think Eric knew anything about him, but, if he did, Alain would have only tried it with him as well. Will I get into trouble for having him as my employee?"

The Boss replied, "That's something for you and the taxman to work out. I don't give a toss, but I have to ask, did you murder Eric or Alain, and you would definitely have had a reason to have a go at Alain."

Art looked a bit shocked, "No! of course I didn't murder anyone! Alain would have sodded off back to France eventually or I'd have stopped taking Becky to the parties. Either way we'd have been away from his clutches."

The Boss asked for Alain's employment records to be sent to his email address and we thanked Art for his time, and I thought we were headed back to the Office, but no.

The Boss was on fire now.

"I reckon we're on a streak, and we should go and see Michael. If the little Frenchie is blackmailing Art and Robin, there's every chance he was also having a go at Michael. Where does he work?"

Micheal had an office down at the end of Hinemoa St, the office end. He had a dozen staff working with him and as far as we knew he was the Boss.

Rolling up to Michael's office and parking, it looked like a flash place. One of those upmarket architects where it cost a grand for the initial interview.

Although not thrilled to see us, Michael welcomed us to his office, and we sat down with a cup of coffee in trendy cups. Everything about the place was flash!

The Boss was on a roll, so he started off.

"Michael. Our other two suspects have both admitted to having Alain as an employee, yet you don't. May I ask, how did you pay the blackmail money to Alain?"

"What blackmail money?"

"The money Alain was grabbing off you for being a closet homosexual."

"I'm sorry, Detective Inspector. Don't know what you are talking about."

"Michael, you do realise that I can get a search warrant and examine all of your bank accounts, don't you?"

"Well maybe that is what you should do, then."

The Boss seemed quite casual as he replied, "Okay, Detective Sergeant, we gave him the chance to come clean. Let's go get the warrant. Maybe we'll come up with something else that Michael doesn't want us to find out about. Can I ask you, Michael. Do you pay the girl in the motel in Malfroy Road by cash or is it by way of a company cheque?"

Michael struggled for a moment with a decision he had to make, "Okay, Inspector, you called my bluff. I've been paying Alain for a few weeks. No it's more like three months, now. I give him a grand once a month and it comes out of my secret cash drawer. The missus doesn't know about it yet so you can leave that out of any conversations we might have in the future. What else do you want to know?"

"Did you kill Alain or Eric?"

"God, no. I'd just got used to paying Alain. Maybe I might have done something about him but, you know what, I was glad when the little sod got topped. It fairly freed me up from paying the little bastard!"

The Boss asked for any bank records pertaining to the payments, but Michael was equally frank. "I just said I paid the sod in cash. I have an accountant that does my books, and he is straight as an arrow. If I was doing anything dodgy he would have been on to it like a flash."

The Boss thanked him for his honesty and said that was it for the time being. We hopped in the Boss's motor and went back to our office.

I reckoned we had a good morning and I had learned a few more things about asking questions of suspects.

When we got back, we filled the Sarge in and he also congratulated the Boss. The we sat down and had lunch while discussing the morning's progress.

The general feeling was that we now had three suspects for Alain's murder and probably the same three suspects for the murder of Eric.

It was the Sarge who first suggested it, "What if, and this is hypothetical, what if Alain knew who did Eric in and he was putting an extra squeeze on that lad?"

With that thought in our brain we redoubled our thinking.

'Only Michael was paying in cash. Easy to increase the amount if you're paying in cash.'

'If it was Robin and Estelle, she would have to know about it to make the extra payments.'

'Art had a thing about not being found out he was a closet gay. Would that be enough if Alain put the extra squeeze on Art?'

We all agreed we had a motive for killing Alain but not for killing Eric. Yet someone had come back to the party when everyone had left and killed Eric. Or if we were to go with Mike the pathologist, it might have been a sex and strangulation thing gone wrong.

The Boss went to see if the 'Employment' details for Alain had come though yet. They had so he added it to the file. Then he got a call from the big Boss. The big Boss said he wanted to him in his office the next day at 9.00. The Boss said he would be there and wondered aloud what had got into the Boss's knickers this late in the day. It was a rhetorical question so none of us answered. At 5.00 we all went home and enjoyed a quiet night, although I couldn't help thinking about what we had uncovered with our three suspects. I thought it increased their motivation to kill Alain now he had the whole blackmail thing going. I pondered a bit more on the Sarge's suggestion about Alain having something extra on one of our three suspects but I didn't recall seeing any extra payments going in to Alain's account just in the last few weeks.

Chapter 11

Wednesday

In bright and early I wanted to check some of the background with our three suspects. But first I needed to do some detective work on the arson case. I sat down with the report and perused it line by line. The inspector did mention that the arsonist had been a little more circumspect with his use of the accelerant, which was petrol, again. This time he had not left a petrol tank at the scene. The last time he had and I remembered the inspector saying the guy was an amateur and had probably been surprised at how quickly the fire had taken hold. I gave the video to the Sarge for him to have a look at first. Theni I turned my attention to the murder case.

Had our suspects been in trouble before? Anything Homosexual of note? Had any of them been in tax trouble before since they had not had an issue with paying their blackmail money to 'Employees'?

The Boss was in fairly early and doing something in his office. I should note he was not in a great mood. It was hosing down outside and he was already wet from dashing to the station back door. Now he would have to go over to the big Boss's office and he would get wet again. Like I said, he was not in a great mood. He said he was checking out what the big Boss wanted but couldn't come up with anything he hadn't done. Not sufficient for the big Boss's tone of voice when he had called the day before.

The Sarge and I wished him luck for his meeting with the big Boss and then we got on with our day.

At a little after 10.00 the Boss was back, and he had a face like thunder!

He called the Sarge and I into his office and then he thought better of it and also called the two DCs in as well.

"Thanks to your success rates the Boss has a new plan for our office. Starting in about six weeks our entire office will move back over the road. He reckons it will take that long to get the alterations done to accommodate our new set up."

The Boss's opening statement floored us all, but then the Boss said, "It gets better. First off, he congratulated me on taking my office to a new level. That put me on the back foot until he told me his plan. Oh, then he asked me if we were making any progress with our murder cases. He knew we weren't, so it made it easier for him to go with his new plan. Starting when we move over there, we are expected to run a 24-hour shift rotation from Thursday until Sunday night. The new shift times will be 8am till 5pm. 4pm till 1.00 am and midnight till 9.00 am. We'll also have to cover Saturday and Sunday days. He reckons he's giving me three new DCs to facilitate the new roster. He repeated what he had said about the three new DC's. As if I haven't got enough to do without babysitting new Detective Constables who are still wet behind the ears! Then he went on about modern policing methods, but I wasn't listening too well. Unofficially he reckons we will function better as a team if we are over the road and under his wing, as it were."

Tim Cross interjected, "We're doing alright as a bloody team without his interference!"

The Boss looked pained," Don't you reckon I might have mentioned that fact to him? No, his mind is set and that's what we have in our future. Sorry, Mark. He reckons you're still up for a transfer which means he can promote one of his bloody minions to be my DS and report everything back to him. Sarge, you'll still be under our watch, but you might have to cover the duty desk once in a while. That means the main desk which means you'll eventually be sucked out of our reach. Gentlemen, he is the Boss of all of us so I would welcome any of your thoughts that I can comfortably take back to him."

The Boss looked defeated, the two DCs were uncertain. I did know that Dave Powell reckoned we should be covering all shifts so he wouldn't be an ally to us. Tim Cross looked teed off. The Sarge was thinking about the news. Then it dawned on him that I was off somewhere else on a transfer, so he asked me, across the room, how long I had known about a transfer possibility. I told him it had been mentioned a couple of weeks ago, but it depended on whether the Boss had a decent holiday. It appears he had not!

"Who is coming in here?" asked Tim Cross.

"I don't know but it will probably be the records people. HR and the like, maybe the pay office," said the Boss.

There were a lot more comments, almost all of which were negative in their nature. But as the Boss said, once the big Boss had made his mind up it was a done deal.

The Sarge was especially disappointed. He'd had almost eight years as the Sarge for the CIB and it somehow suited him to be the elder statesman of a group of relative rookies. Now he would be absorbed into the general police stream of events. The Boss asked me to hang on for a moment as the rest of the team left his office.

"I really tried for you to be a part of the new team, but the Boss is adamant you are on the move. He told me to tell you it was on, your transfer. But I told him it was over to him to formally advise you. Expect a call over the next few days. Sorry, Mark. I did my best."

"Thanks, Boss. Don't worry about it. Now, do I sell my place in Holland St, or do I hang on to it for when I retire? Or do I retire now and get a job somewhere else? I've got twenty plus years in. I could get a pension. Oh well, that will give me something to think about for a few days."

"Mark," the Boss replied, "You're too good a copper to walk away. Don't do anything without talking to me first."

I left the Boss's office and walked straight into the Sarge. As he was waiting right outside the Boss's office it wasn't that hard to miss him.

"So, how long have you known about this transfer and when were you going to tell me about it?" That was uppermost on the Sarge's mind.

I wasn't really in the mood, but Sarge and I had been friends since before I left England.

"Like I said the big Boss was thinking about it while he was on holiday. It seems like he didn't enjoy his holiday very much."

The Sarge then surprised me, "Well if you get a nice new place to hang up your hat, see if there's a place for a Sarge as well. I can't see myself settling in under the big Boss. I don't speak his PC language and I definitely don't speak any Māori!"

The Boss suggested I go off and do some busy work. That means I should go and get myself another coffee and have a bit of quiet time while I did some thinking about my situation.

I have to say that my Boss was showing a lot more leadership and compassion than the Big Boss was doing, and he was doing a damn sight more for team spirit, as well.

I got back to the office, Tim, and Dave, the two DCs were both thinking about their future. Was it time to push for a transfer. They knew the Boss would give them excellent references. Neither of them saw their future as being that rosy under the big Boss's leadership. When I say leadership, I should add under the big Boss's direct leadership! The big Boss was known for doing things by the book. Our own Boss was more supportive if we occasionally colored outside the lines, and sometimes you had to color outside the lines to get the job done!

I sat at my desk and wondered what to do about my future. Then I decided thinking about it wouldn't help so I would put the time to better use and look at the murder case. I pulled up the files on the cases and sat down to trawl through them again. I must have looked at the files on at least a dozen separate occasions and I soon fell into the trap of just reading them as they were. The only new items were the employment records of Alain by two of the suspects. I glanced at the employment records, but they were insufficient to hold my attention any more than the rest of the files in the case, or cases.

I wondered about going out and visiting one of my CI's. Maybe I'd go and see Angel. I hadn't seen her in a while. With that thought in mind I redoubled my attention with the murder cases. It was not a lot of use; it was all stuff I had read a dozen times or more. It brought up lunchtime and went and got a Subway sandwich. Sitting down with the Sarge we commiserated about our future over lunch, and he said he would be sad to leave Rotorua, if it came to the crunch. And his missus, Huia would be even more teed off. After lunch I got on the phone to Angel and then Tiff and they were both not answering their phone. I ended up giving Janet a call and she was very keen that I go and see her.

Arranging a time for later on, I wondered what to do next. I decided to go and see Ronnie. If nothing else, it would pass the time. I rang Ronnie and he was up for a visit, so I went round to see him.

Ronnie was moaning about the rival gang in town trying to pinch his customers. Without letting too much out, he was telling me about the problems he was having. It seemed that our work with Jacko had resulted in him losing over half of his team of 'security guards' and anyone who applied to work for him needed to get security clearance before they even started to work for him. That was bad news for Jacko but conversely it was good news for Ronnie. His monthly income had gone up by around forty percent since Jacko had taken his hit. Anyone with a record was almost automatically excluded from his team. Anyone with a drug history was also banned from working for him. Now Jacko was left employing only real security men who would not get involved with supplying drugs to the residents of halfway motels etc. I can only assume that Ronnie had picked up quite a bit of extra trade from these fall outs. Now it seems that the rival gang was making an effort to recover some of these customers either by brute force or with a bit of a discount on their prices.

Here's something you should think about. The drug suppliers are supplying a need. They have customers who feel they actually need the drugs. If we cut off the drug supply, we would be left with a few hundred people all desperate for drugs. Desperate enough to commit a serious crime. That's the reality of what we have to deal with. Sometimes it is better to have a drug supplier than have a few people bordering on desperation to get their fix! By knowing what and who we were dealing with, although it may appear distasteful, it did give us some control of the overall situation.

I didn't feel sorry for Ronnie but to show my face I did have to at least appear sympathetic. While it was good to have a brew with Ronnie, I was also mindful that I had time booked with Janet. Leaving Ronnie, I was off to Janet's place in Malfroy Road.

The last time I had been there we had something of a lovers tiff. Not that we were lovers as such. She wanted to talk about the case, and I wanted to have some fun. We had compromised but it wasn't the best of times we had together.

Today she remembered the reason for my visit, and she was 'accommodating'. I hate to use the expression 'half time break' but there came a time when we did have a talk. She asked me how we were getting on and I gave her a brief update on the case. Don't think badly of me, as she had been involved in the early stages. I told her about what we had discovered with Alain blackmailing the three guys. She reckoned that did not surprise her. Also she reckoned that Lesley perhaps knew more than she was letting on and to be wary about Robin's wife Estelle. She had a cold heart, and she was skilled in the use of sex to get what she wanted. When I pressed Janet for details, she said she just had a feeling about Lesley and Estelle. Call it woman's intuition if I wanted. I did say that was not a lot of use in a murder trial then we got involved in some other stuff.

It was close enough to 4.30 so I went home and called it a day. I really had to get my head back into the caseload or it would affect my input. Also it may affect my chances of a decent transfer, when it happened.

Thursday

In at my usual time and, as always, the Sarge beat me in. We had our coffee and I asked if the Sarge had mentioned a possible move to his wife, Huia. In summary she was not in favour of a move. She was also no longer a big fan of the big Boss.

The two DCs were getting on with the calls requiring CIB input and I had the morning to do what I wanted.

The first case I looked at was the arsonist. He had done a couple of schools by now - Western Heights Intermediate and Ngongotaha Primary. Sadly, it looked like it would be one of those cases where we had to wait for the guy to set another place on fire and we could add that to his list of charges. We still liked him for the three cases of weed spray on the sports grounds. Again we would have to catch him first and see what he would own up to. I'd had another word with the Police Psych guy this week. He reckoned it was likely to be a guy that was single or in a bad marriage. Probably shorter in stature and he definitely liked reading about himself in the papers. So far there had been nothing in the national papers. That was likely to be his real aim in making the nationals. He already had some success with the local paper. As we had nothing really to go on, I turned my attention to the murders.

CIB work is really quite boring and nothing like you see on the TV. I pulled up the files on the two murders and prepared to go over them again. This time I was being a little more methodical in my approach. I was looking at every piece of paper (on the computer screen) as an individual item. By mid-morning I was still only a quarter of the way through the file, but it served the purpose of relieving my boredom and stopped me dozing my way through the file. By midafternoon I had worked my way through around two thirds of the file. Occasionally, I had to stop and look at the papers that Alain's sister had dumped on us but is still had nothing that could remotely be described as a lead. If anything, looking at a real piece of paper made a change from looking at the computer screen, so it helped to keep me occupied and alert.

By 5.00 I had just about finished with the file, and I only had to look at Alain's employment records. I hung on to look at them. There was something there that didn't quite add up, but I was, by now, too tired to be bothered looking or thinking about them anymore. I went home and promised myself a quiet night. I tried my best, but I couldn't help thinking I was still missing something, and the answer was in the file. It was something I would look at tomorrow, probably. With the whole transfer thing, my mind was not terribly centered on Rotorua's problems. While trying to get to sleep I turned my thoughts to whether I would quit the force and take the pension or where I would contemplate as a transfer. My thoughts went back to the three years I had in Napier nick. They had been fun, and with that thought I eventually dozed off.

Friday

It hit me around 3.00 am that I should be taking a closer look, and a real look at Alain's employment records. The previous day I had been taking a cursory glance at them as I wound down from my full day of looking at all of the Boss's files. Lying in my warm bed I easily resisted the temptation to go into the office, but I was in there a little after seven am and I even beat the Sarge in! It was a murky day outside so I was quite looking forward to a day inside the office.

Try as I might I could see nothing wrong with the employment records, yet my gut instinct was telling me I was missing something. Finally it hit me!

Robin and Estelle had marked Alain down as leaving their service and the time stamp was noted as 8.37am on the Saturday. Art had not noted Alain as leaving until the Monday morning. How did Robin and Estelle know he had left, or was dead, on Saturday morning?

I couldn't wait for the Boss to get in and he did not arrive until after 9.00 He had been over to the new station and the big Boss had been showing him what was to be our new offices. It was a courtesy by the big Boss, but it did show to all that the big Boss made the decisions. My Boss was suitably indifferent to the big Boss's grandiose schemes, but he did say it wasn't that bad of a set up, However, he thought it seemed a bit of a shame to knock around what the builders had done in building the new station just a couple of years before. The big Boss was undeterred. He was getting his way!

I waited for the Boss to finish telling his story about the big Boss before I showed him what I had discovered. He took it carefully and considered what I had found. Then he shared my jubilation and we plotted how we would get Robin and/or Estelle to confess to their parts.

We had to assume that Robin had been the one that was having sex with Eric and Robin was certainly strong enough to rig the suicide up. But Alain? The Boss and I were on different sides with Alain's murder. I fancied Estelle and the Boss fancied Robin. We planned our strategy in that we would get them both into the interview rooms over the road at the new station. We could get the Sarge to look in on the interview. We would ask them both to come in and then separate them into two interview rooms.

Once we had the mechanics of the interview sorted out, the rest was not that hard.

Robin and Estelle came into the new station, and we separated them, which did not go down well with either of them.

Our first interview was with Estelle. We asked her if the employment records for Alain had been doctored or anything like that. For once, the Boss let me handle the whole interview. Estelle kept looking at the Boss as he was the one who usually asked the questions. I have to hand it to the Boss, the way he was delegating the interviewing to me was a big plus, but it also gave him the opportunity to occasionally interject with a question. It certainly kept Robin and

Estelle on their toes as they never really knew who would ask the next question.

Estelle was adamant that the employment records were for the taxman so they couldn't be rigged or anything dodgy.

"So, Estelle, I read these records correctly and it appears you made the entry noting that Alain had left your employ at 8.37am on the Saturday morning."

"Yes, I was in bright and early that day. I wanted to get everything ready for the accountant, so I went in on the Saturday. It's not unusual for me to put in a Saturday. What's your point?"

I continued, "Thanks for the clarification, Estelle. May I ask how come you knew that Alain had left your employ at 8.37 am when the person finding the body did not discover it until at least an hour later. Why is that do you think?"

Estelle knew she had been caught but she did try to wriggle her way out of it. "I don't know. Perhaps the clock is wrong in the office. I mean the computer clock, obviously. Perhaps Lesley rang me with the news. That's it. Lesley rang me. We are close friends."

The Boss gave me a nudge with his knee. I continued," Estelle, we are going to talk with Robin now. So far you have given us three reasons why you should not be guilty of this crime. Perhaps you could just pick one and then we'll use that one for your statement."

With that we got up and left Estelle to mellow or confess. Outside in the corridor the Boss high fived me and said I had improved my interrogation techniques. He congratulated me on my closing technique and how I had left Estelle on the hook, thinking about which answer she would give regarding the time of the entry on Alain's record. The lessons he had been giving me must be working out well! The Sarge was also out in the corridor, and he was thrilled for us.

"She's sat in the interview room, and she knows she's caught. Well done, DS. Well done!"

Next, we reconvened in Robins interview room. The Sarge was in his usual spot behind the one-way mirror.

At the Boss's suggestion I took the lead.

"Robin, we would like to talk to you about the night of Eric's murder. That would be the early morning after the party when you came back alone."

I could feel the Boss alongside me swelling with pride. His interview techniques were playing out well.

"So who said I even came back?"

That was unexpected and I was just a little flummoxed.

The Boss spoke, "Alain?"

"The little French bastard! That was the whole reason for me paying his money."

I now had a better line of questioning in the Boss's style.

"Robin, we have the coroner's report that the victim was strangled before being strung up to look like a suicide. I'd welcome your input."

"It was Eric! He had this asphyxiation thing going on. You know, he like to be choked a bit. Said it made it better for him. When he stopped responding to things I panicked. Estelle was out in the car, and I got her in. It was her idea to make it look like suicide. Yes, I did it, but it was her idea. During the whole time that bugger Alain was watching us. He'd wanted to go and see if Estelle wanted some comforting but by the time, he got dressed she was inside, and we were... Oh God. What happens now?" He dropped his head into his hands.

The Boss spoke next, "Would you excuse us, Robin. We need to confer for a moment."

Outside in the corridor the Boss was ecstatic.

"You've got them, both. Now let's go and have a brew. Let them stew for five minutes then they'll be ready to tell us everything."

The Sarge was blown away with the results," I told you they were both bloody liars!"

The Boss was quite chirpy, "You say that about every crim in the nick. Come on. I reckon you should get your wallet out and buy us a brew," with that he led the way upstairs to the cafeteria."

When we got upstairs the Boss let the Sarge buy us all a brew and then we sat down.

The Boss let out what had been troubling him for the last couple of days.

"You two are both thinking about jumping ship, aren't you?"

We agreed that retirement was one of the options or a transfer might be another way to go.

"Well, I've got twenty years plus in. Maybe retirement is an option for me as well. I had a word with my wife yesterday and she doesn't really fancy a move out of town. Reckons she won't know anyone unless we all move together. Something to think about, you reckon?"

It was a brief and mainly lighthearted discussion, but I couldn't help but think about it that night as I lay in bed.

Getting back to the Nicholsons, Robin and Estelle. They both confessed to their involvement. Robin had something do with Eric's murder and so did his wife Estelle. Estelle eventually pleaded guilty to Alain's murder. She said she went to Alain to discuss how wrong it was to blackmail Robin. Alain made a suggestion that Estelle could pay off some of the debt by, you know what. He said he would give her marks out of ten. If she performed well, it could save her a few dollars. She reckoned she was so annoyed that she grabbed the first thing she could lay her hands on, which was the pipe that Alain used to answer the door with, him being so alone in a foreign country. He was going towards the bed when she whacked him. After that it became something of a blur. She remembered tossing the pipe into the field on the way back to her car, which was parked at the gate. She reckoned she didn't want to drive up the driveway as it might have alerted Lesley, but after that she doesn't even remember going home and telling Robin about what she had done.

The Boss thought it might be better to get the CP involved with what charges could be laid. Robin and Estelle spent the night in custody and got bail the next day, by which time the Boss had laid the formal charges. I think Robin got charged with death by misadventure or something like that. Estelle got charged with Alain's murder and also being a party to the mock suicide of Eric. I think that charge was something about aspiring to pervert the course of justice.

By half past 4 we were in a celebratory mood and there was talk of us all going out for a few drinks when the big Boss rang me on my direct line. He said he wanted to see me at 9.00 Monday morning. That put paid to our drinks evening but we still decided to make it the next night as by then I would know my fate.

As luck would have it, I was down for the Saturday and the Boss volunteered to cover for me. The Sarge had a word with Tim Cross and before I knew it the Sarge and the Boss and I were going out for a game of golf, with Tim handling the Saturday shift. Tee off at 11.00am and we could just go as a threesome which meant the Sarge could have a whack with a few balls without any other player getting upset.

Chapter 12

The three of us went out on Saturday at 11.00 and we were blessed with no one else bothering us. The Boss and I played a semi-serious game, and the Sarge had a few whacks from 100 yards off the green and then putting out. I have to say that the Sarge was natural. Maybe it's because of the lessons the Boss and I were giving him, but he did have a natural swing that we couldn't emulate.

I believe I beat the Boss and we had a drink in the bar afterwards. The Sarge commented that 'This beats getting the boat out of the water every time you want to go fishing.'

So the Sarge had thought a little more seriously about taking up golf, sufficient to take a day off the next week and go for some lessons with the pro at Springfield. I should be on commission with the pro!

That Saturday night we went out and got just a bit merry. That doesn't quite cover it and we got the Boss to do his trick on the squad car to either breathalyze us or drive us home. During the course of the evening I believe we discussed the benefits of us all going to a new office but then we reckoned the big Boss would not allow us all to go together. So we had another drink and the evening went on. It was a very merry evening!

Monday

Monday morning came and I was in at the usual time. I had my coffee and all the while the Sarge was telling me to stay calm when I was with the big Boss. I had every intention of staying calm for at least the first minute when I walked into his office.

There is a protocol with any person who is of a higher rank. First off you don't sit down unless invited. He kept me standing while he finished off some paperwork. It may have been only for a couple of minutes, but it still irked me, just a little. He was being a sod just for the sake of it!

When I was finally invited to sit down the big Boss went on about what a wonderful career a job with the Police was. The chance to travel and be in offices anywhere in the country etc. He did dwell on how long the murder case was taking but he soon shut up when I told him the case had been solved due to my efforts. That was a mistake. He then went on about how a career officer such as I should embrace the challenge of a change of office and a change of rank perhaps.

I was already sick of the talk he was giving, and I was waiting for him to get to the point. It might have taken ten minutes, but he finally told me I was overdue for a transfer, and I would have no difficulty selling my house etc. There is a phrase in any uniformed ranks and that is silent insubordination. I was not going to give him the satisfaction of accusing me of anything but the respect his rank should always be accorded.

When he had concluded his little pep talk, I asked if there was anything else. When he replied in the negative, I stood up and left his office.

I believe he may have thought I was going to argue with him, but I wasn't going to give him that satisfaction. I was due for a transfer sometime in the next three months as per the rules. That gave me time to sell my house and look for new accommodation where I was to be transferred. I was still thinking I might retire and look for a job in Rotorua but that was on the backburner.

I have to thank the Boss for this. When I got back to our temporary office, I told the Sarge everything that had been said by the big Boss. To be honest I was hurting just a little. I'd just closed a big case, a double murder case and all I had received from my big Boss was a pat on the back and a 'this will help you in your new job' speech.

Yeah, I was just a bit teed off.

The Boss handed everything on to the CP. Robin & Estelle got bail, which surprised me, but the CP didn't argue too hard as they had to get their business affairs in order and we did have them dead to rights!

One thing that I didn't expect was a letter from the big Boss a couple of days after my interview with him. I should say I expected a letter from the Big Boss, but the contents were not what I expected. It seems he'd had a rethink about my position, and I was no longer on for a transfer. The letter said I had a future with his division and to keep up the sterling work I was doing with my Boss. He said he expected great things from us.

I knew straight away that the Boss had gone into bat for me and he must have thought I was too valuable to let go from our division. Or something like that!

I marched into the Boss's office and showed him the letter. I thanked him for his efforts. Perhaps I had not thanked him well enough before, but he said it was the least he could do for a good copper who showed promise.

Now, as I said, I always like to tell the reader what happened with the sentences etc. Estelle owned up to Alain's murder and she also managed to convince the jury that Robin had sod all to do with stringing Eric up. Something about him being too upset at his friend's death or something like that. She got a good brief who convinced the jury that Alain's actions in asking for sex had disturbed the brain thing of Estelle. Anyway, she got off with 12 years inside. Robin got a hung jury. Maybe he had a few of the jury who were modern in their thinking or maybe they were that way inclined. Whatever, he got a hung jury, and a retrial is pending. Estelle is still trying to do the books for Robin's company from her prison cell, but she is having some difficulty with access to the internet. I can't think why?

Art and his poor partner got an audit from the taxman. As I understand it, Art's partner was well displeased about Art having Alain on the books as an employee. I can't see that partnership lasting too long if I correctly interpret what the Boss is telling me about what is being said in the Rotary drinking sessions.

Lesley put her place on the market, and it sold fairly quickly although I don't remember seeing anything about a couple of murders happening there. Last I heard, she was heading up to Auckland to be with her sister. I'd probably think the swingers market is a bit more buoyant up there, but that's not for me to speculate.

Epilogue

Dave Smith and Colin Woods were having their weekly game of golf along with Mark Hammell at the Springfield Golf club. Colin and Dave were both on top of the hill that juts out into the tenth fairway. Mark had put his tee shot into the eighth fairway. He'd fairly walloped the daylights out of his tee shot which had started well and then turned into a bit of a hook shot. The Boss reckoned it was going backwards when it landed, the hook was so pronounced! so while Colin and Dave waited by their balls Mark was off getting ready to make a recovery shot back onto the tenth fairway.

Dave and Colin chatted while they were waiting for Mark.

"What do you reckon we should do about Ronnie and the mob?"

"Well we either keep telling Ronnie who the BP's are supplying to, or we have a go at the Black Power lads and tell them to cut us in. For me I'd be happy to let the Mob keep pushing them out," said Dave.

"What was our cut last month?"

"Up over nine grand."

"That's not too bad. Maybe we'll keep with the Mob and give it a month or so more? Best not to be too greedy and kill off a cash cow. Hey, I had Mark into my office last week. Reckons he has to thank me for the Boss changing his mind. I had sod all to do with the Boss changing his mind. So I reckon it must have been you! Did you go and have a word with him, my Boss?"

"Yes, I might have mentioned it to him." This was said while Dave was wondering what club he would need for the shot to go over the valley and then up to the elevated green. It was a slightly uphill lie and Dave would have to take that into account when judging which club he wanted to use.

"So I was right, you do know where the bodies are buried."

"In England it's called knowing which skeleton is in which cupboard. A Sarge told me once always have something on someone. It pays dividends when you are in a tight corner. This time it did work out alright, for Mark."

"So you do have something on the Boss?"

"I've got something on most people I've had the pleasure of working with."

"But not me, right!"

"One of these days I might have to tell you about it, but today we're enjoying our golf. Hang on, Mark has taken his shot and the bugger's on the green. What a tinny bastard, but it will count when we decide who is buying the beers tonight. You're away next, I reckon you might go with a six iron, but you might consider a four iron if you're feeling brave. Mark is already on the green for two."

With that thought we will leave the lads enjoying their game of golf.

Police series

A series about crime in 'Rotorua'

Book1 <u>The Panel</u>

It seems there is a 'panel' of people in Rotorua who decides if the local court system is giving a fair shake to the local criminals. If they get off lightly there may be further retribution available.

Book 2 <u>The Party</u>

A party takes place out in Hamurana area and the next day there is a murder case at the same address. Coincidence? Or is there more than meets the eye?

Book 3 <u>The Judge</u>

We appear to have a moral guardian at work. Then there is also another guy committing the same crime. Coincidence or not?

Book 4 <u>The War</u>

It's finally happened, and a gang war breaks out. The last thing the Police need is for someone else to get involved. And the last thing the Police need is always exactly what happens!

Book 5 <u>The payoff.</u>

It's a time when people need to decide who is on their side. And who can be let go? It's time for all friendships to be tested!

<u>Other work by the same Author</u>

Soul Purpose

Vol 1 & 11 & 111

A fiction work with something of a twist

He has returned.

The subtitle is "and it's so not what you think" Probably one of the most fun books I have written and probably the most amusing. The Son of God has returned, and he finds the world is in something of a state. Partly because of what he said and did a couple of thousand years ago on his last visit here. Yeah, it's all a bit confused now he is back. Let's see how he deals with it!

Mickey Carter: An angel with L-plates

It's funny and set in South Manchester. It's easy being an angel. Isn't it?

I have Angels at my table.

An interesting story set in England as natural disasters occur and somehow the higher levels of heaven are involved.

Danny Casanova's legacy

A fun story centred around a young guy's first venture into the world of grown-ups and doing what grown-ups do. Or at least trying to!

Time and time again.

A book about past life experiences. Interestingly it only deals with past lives on planet earth.

About the Author

Andy has been writing for the last twenty years and has written a number of books over a wide variety of genre. His first book Sold over 5000 copies and he continues to write on whatever the mood takes him. Currently he is finishing Books on the crime scene in Rotorua, New Zealand. As always his books are not meant to be taken seriously. If you haven't laughed today, read one of Andy's books!